Luke's Apocalypse

Zero Day

A.P. Shepherd

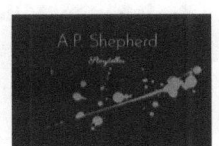

For my Sophia

Chapter 1

Luke

* * *

Rain was pounding hard against the windowpane. Luke tossed and turned, trying to find sleep again, but every time the thunder rumbled, Archie whined. Luke buried his head deeper under the covers and pillows. It didn't help. He couldn't turn off the thoughts of his argument with Kate. And now, the storm was doing its best to break through the windows, and Archie was carrying on like a scared puppy...

Then there was another sound too, though. It was out of place somehow. Archie growled, deep and low in his throat. Luke froze for a moment.

Was that a scream?

"It's only the wind, boy. Easy."

Blurry-eyed, Luke glanced at the red numbers of the old clock sitting on the dresser, the same clock he'd had since he was a small boy. He didn't know how long those things were supposed to last, but he had it for as long as he could remember. Luke loved that old clock and never once thought about replacing it. The vivid memory of waking up to those bright red numbers to get ready for school came rushing back to him. Oh, and to the smell of mom's bacon and eggs cooking in the kitchen. He missed those days — he missed Mom.

"Great, now I'm hungry," he grumbled. *Man, was it really that long ago?*

But he remembered it like yesterday.

Luke stretched and ran his fingers through his messy mop of hair. Kate had been after him to get it cut, but he didn't want to. He liked it. Things were so different now, working from home so much - he could almost get away with it. Almost.

Crack! Boom!

Luke and Archie both jumped! That one got his heart going.

"Crap, that was a big one! It scared me too, boy. Man, it's coming down out there."

Luke remembered when Archie was just an 8-week old fur ball, the day he brought him home. It rained hard that day too. Little Archie trembled and whined and tried to crawl up into Luke's jacket to hide. Luke melted inside when he did that, and he pulled over to the side of the road to cuddle with Archie until the rain stopped. He felt such a strong need to protect him and make him feel safe. It was in that moment that he somehow knew they would have an unbreakable bond. Now, a year later, and Archie was just about his best friend in the entire world.

"Get up here, you big baby," Luke said.

The old antique bed creaked and groaned when the 90-pound German Shepherd hopped up in one fluid motion.

Archie licked Luke right on the mouth, but with that big boloney tongue of his, it was more like the entire front of his face. Luke hurried his forearm across his face.

"Yeah, I love you too, boy."

Bark!

He thought about the book he'd been working on and wondered if he could get some writing done tonight since he couldn't sleep.

With his and Kate's argument on his mind? He doubted it. Maybe he would still try.

Kate really got him going last night. His plans to go hunting with Jonah upset her more than he expected. But Luke wanted to go, and this year he was planning to take Archie. On second thought, maybe he'd be better off talking to Jonah instead. Perhaps they could find a different weekend. Thanksgiving was a bad time to leave Kate to go off on a hunting trip. Especially since she had her heart set on them spending it with her parents together this year.

"I'm in a no-win situation, Big Bear," he said to Archie.

Luke loved Thanksgiving and Christmas. He got that love of the Holidays from his mom. She always made it a special time for the family, with all the decorations, her baking, and playing her favorite Christmas music. Ever since he was a kid, it was the time of year that he could hardly wait for. But this year, he was going to make someone unhappy no matter what he did.

Luke hated being all wishy-washy... His dad used to always say, "Son, a man has to be strong, make up his mind about a thing, and stick to it!" That was a pet peeve of his dad's. Luke guessed he sort of inherited it himself.

I don't think I had a choice.

He pursed his lips.

Crack!

The wind howled outside, and Luke couldn't remember a time that it rained this hard.

"I need some coffee."

The moment Luke stood, the lights flickered.

"No, no, no... please, no!" Luke pleaded with the lights. That always helped, didn't it?

Well, that would be great, he thought, the lights going out too. The drawings he'd been working on were due today. Mr. Blake was pretty adamant about that. Luke had been procrastinating too much. He had been spending too much time on his book these last few days. Well that, and with Kate.

Crack! Scream!

"Okay, that wasn't the wind! What the heck was that?"

His phone rang.

Luke almost jumped out of his skin!

"Son of a...!"

"Hello?"

"Hey, bro."

"Jonah, hey. Man, it's 3 AM. Why are you calling me at this crazy hour? Are you okay? Is something wrong?"

"Luke, turn on the news! You're not gonna believe what's going on."

"Yea sure - okay, hang on."

Luke grabbed the remote from the night table, turned on the TV and tuned it to the local independent news station. After the last Presidential election - he despised TV, and especially the news, but it was the only one he could stomach anymore.

Fire... Fire everywhere, and there were so many flashing lights of firetrucks and police cars.

Luke's breath hitched. There seemed to be a large swath of land covered in flames, and there was a lot of smoke. The news woman was saying something about a plane crash, but between the rain outside, and the sounds from all around her, it was difficult to understand her. A banner across the bottom of the screen confirmed what he thought he'd heard her saying. *"A Midwestern Airlines Flight has crashed near a large residential area in Mason City."*

The area looked familiar... But there was so much smoke and activity that he couldn't be sure. Then the view shifted and zeroed in on a couple of paramedics with a woman who appeared to be in terrible shape. She was frantic and struggling as the paramedics were trying to get her strapped down to a gurney. Much of her face and neck looked to be covered in blood, and her clothes were tattered and burned. But it was her eyes that drew Luke in. Her eyes were open wide and appeared to be completely black, with no white at all. She writhed and fought and looked to be trying to get free from the paramedics.

"Man, what is this?" he asked Jonah.

"Bro, this is crazy. They were saying the plane went down, because passengers were going nuts onboard. The pilot radioed in that passengers were attacking each other. There was a lot of screaming on his radio conversation with the tower. Then, the plane just went down. It was supposed to land in Des Moines."

"If I didn't know you better, Jonah, I'd say you were full of crap!"

"No man, it's what they've been talking about for two hours. I tried calling you at least a dozen times since midnight, but the phone lines, or circuits, or whatever, are all jammed up, and I couldn't get through. Luke, this has me a little worried. I can't put my finger on why, a feeling maybe? But there's something about this that's, well... off. Ya know?"

Jonah was the toughest guy Luke ever knew, ever since they were kids. When they played Highschool football together, no one wanted to line up against Jonah. He was a beast and could put just about anyone on the ground. Since then, he only got bigger. If Jonah was worried, then there was something to worry about.

"What do you think's happening? What's got you spooked?" Luke asked.

"I'm not sure, bro, but I've been watching the news since the storm, or whatever, woke me up around 11:30. Then I got a call from Ted, to be ready to come in if he called me back. But from what they've been saying, so far, they've only found two survivors. The paramedics were treating one of them, and she looked like she had gone mad, or maybe she was in so much pain that she couldn't keep it together. Did you see her on the news?"

"Yeah, she sort of freaked me out too," Luke said.

"Well, the second one ran off into the woods behind the large estate homes near Mason City Country Club, across from the big golf course. Several people saw her limp away. And from what they were saying, she was in bad shape, too. I mean, why would anyone do that? Who does that Luke?"

The television news camera panned around to a large supermarket with all the front windows blown out.

"Oh, no... is that...?"

"Yeah man, it is."

"I can't believe it! I was buying groceries there yesterday."

The lights flickered inside the large supermarket and then went black. After that, the entire area, other than all the floodlights and flashing lights from the emergency vehicles, went dark.

Luke's heart beat a little faster. "Jonah, did they say anything about where the flight came in from?"

"No, I don't think they wanted to give out any flight info yet, because of the passengers and their families. Why, man?"

"I don't know. I was just thinking about a story I saw on the News last week. A Ukrainian plane had to make an emergency landing in Turkey, and it showed several passengers being carried off the plane and taken away in ambulances. They looked a lot like the lady on the news with ripped clothes and all bloody. I remember looking for more news on it, but found nothing other than some social media pictures and comments. But all the comments were in Russian or something and I didn't bother after that. Seeing that lady with the paramedics sort of reminded me of that. Did you hear about that?" asked Luke.

"No, but you know me bro, I never watch the news. The only reason I turned it on tonight was because my bedroom started shaking, and then a loud boom rattled my windows. At first I thought it was thunder, but it wasn't like any thunder I'd ever heard before," Jonah said.

At that moment, the news began scrolling new text along the bottom of the screen, saying that the crash site and all the surrounding area were being locked down. Authorities are also asking everyone in the surrounding areas to stay indoors, and to keep all roads clear for emergency vehicles. Luke had turned down the volume to talk to Jonah, so he didn't hear what they were saying.

"Jonah, are you watching this?" Luke asked.

"Yeah man, I guess I'm stuck here with Ted for a while?"

"Do you know what happened to the lady the paramedics were helping? "

"Nah, all I heard on the radio while I was driving over here was that a survivor was being taken to Mercy. I guess that was her. They've just been playing that clip over and over again. But I think they said some people on the ground were hurt too. Hey, I gotta run. Ted's yelling at me to check something. I'll call you later."

"Okay bro, see ya."

The line went silent.

Luke sat there for a minute, staring at the television, his mind racing as he thought about the woman. She was... She was what? He didn't know... But it was something. He had this weird feeling and he couldn't get that look of hers out of his head. It almost seemed like she wasn't real or something. Animated maybe? The look in her eyes mesmerized Luke. Just then, Archie yawned and stretched. That snapped Luke out of his daze. He hadn't noticed until now, but it was quieter outside. The rain was letting up a bit. He thought about calling Kate, but it was way too early in the morning, and besides, what would he say? Still, he wanted to talk to her. He needed to talk to her.

And a moment later, the lights went out.

Chapter 2

Light's Out

* * *

"Well, Big Bear, it's official. I'm screwed if the power doesn't come back on soon."

He would soon learn how right he was. Because it would be a long time before the lights came back on. A very long time...

"Come on, let's go figure out how we can make some coffee. I can't even think about what to do next without that. We'll get you a snack too. You deserve it after that crazy storm."

Bark!

Luke touched the flashlight app on his phone and shone the light towards the bedroom door. The light reflected off the old hardwood floors, and dimly into the pitch black hallway. It was very dark inside the house. Spooky dark. And it could be considered a spooky old house to begin with. It wasn't to Luke though - he'd grown up in this old house. It was his grandmother's house, and her mother's house before that. Grams left it to Luke when she died, and he loved this old house. He spent most summers here as a young boy and then moved in with his grandparents when his mom and dad died in a car accident when Luke was only 16; he was now 27. Mom loved cooking with Grams and gardening with her in the big garden out back. Luke had a lot of good memories growing up here. It was an original Victorian built in 1901, but it was still in great shape. It was a big house, and though it creaked and groaned just about everywhere, it was a sturdy old house, and it was home.

The wind was still blowing despite the rain having stopped. Luke reached and found his warm socks at the foot of the bed. He picked up one, pulled it on, but then, as he tried to pick up the second one, Archie grabbed it and started playing tug of war with him.

"Hey boy, drop it. Please don't tear it. This is my last pair of warm socks that don't have Archie holes." Archie hesitated for a moment, stared at Luke with playful eyes, and then, after a moment longer, let go. Though Luke could tell that he really didn't want to.

Archie was very young and playful, but he was well-trained. Luke had worked with him for hours and hours every week. That was one of Luke's favorite times of the day - when he could break away from work and spend that time with Archie. It was Archie's happiest time as well. He was always so completely focused on Luke during that time - and his eyes never left Luke. Luke didn't know that dogs could be that way, so focused on their master like that. Not until he got Archie. They had a small family dog when he was a young boy, and she always greeted Luke with a wagging tail and kisses, and Luke loved her a lot, but she really wasn't *Luke's* dog. Not like this.

Archie dropped Luke's sock, and then laid down flat on the bed with his paws in front of him, and his face flat between them. With a slight raise of his brow, he moved his eyes up to look at Luke. It was that sweet look that Luke loved the most. Archie was definitely feeling better now since the thunder stopped.

"Thanks, Big Bear, and thanks for *slobbering* all over it. I really appreciate that," Luke said, ruffling the soft fur on his head while pulling on his soggy sock.

Bark!

9

Luke stood, and stretched, a good long stretch, along with an enormous yawn. The floor creaked as usual, but he was so used to that sound that it barely registered, and Luke started towards the hallway outside of his bedroom. He couldn't get over how dark it was. There wasn't the faintest of light through any window, no moonlight, nothing. Just blackness. That small glow from his phone felt like the only light in the whole world at that moment. Archie jumped down from the bed too with a loud thump and started towards the bedroom door. Luke stopped at the dresser next to the door, picked up a box of matches, and lit the candle that was standing there. Losing power in this old house happened more often than he liked, so he had learned to keep plenty of candles and flashlights around. Somehow, lighting the candle made Luke feel better. It cast a warm glow, but it was a kind of spooky glow, with the wind still howling outside through the large maple trees. He picked up the flashlight sitting there and clicked it on. Nothing. He clicked it off and on a few more times, but still there was no light. Then he banged it against his thigh, but that didn't help either. "Great," he huffed. He had forgotten to recharge the batteries after the last few times he'd used it.

Leaving the candle sitting on the dresser, Luke moved into the dark hallway. He dropped his phone in surprise, when it suddenly started buzzing in his hand.

"Crap!" Luke half yelled, half whispered. Then looked at the phone lying face-up on the floor and saw that it was Kate. In an instant, reasons she would call at this crazy hour flooded his mind, and none of them were good. He reached down and picked it up and answered it.

"Hey Katie, you okay?" he said with mild irritation. Not because it was Kate, but because he felt silly for being so jumpy.

"Hi baby, should I be asking you the same thing?"

Hearing the way she said, 'baby', made Luke relax a bit.

"No, I'm okay. I just dropped my phone when you called. Guess I'm kinda jumpy with this crazy storm, and the lights being out and all."

"Your lights are out again?"

"Yeah, I was lighting candles and using my phone as a flashlight when it rang and buzzed in my hand."

"Oh, Luke, I'm sorry," she said, as she tried to suppress her big grin.

"No you're not. I can hear you smiling."

Then Kate started outright giggling.

"It's just, I can picture you walking around that big old spooky house of yours with your flashlight phone in the dark, and then jumping and throwing it when it rings... It's too perfect," she laughed.

Then Luke started laughing. Then they were both laughing. Their laughter grew, and then they were both laughing so hard that they couldn't speak. It was that sort of contagious laughing that you sometimes get, and just can't stop, no matter how hard you try. And the harder you try, the harder you laugh.

After what felt like minutes, and with watery eyes, they both stopped and caught their breath beneath a few remaining giggles, and then Kate said, "Luke, I'm sorry I got upset with you last night. It was selfish of me to make you choose between me and going on your hunting trip with Jonah. You should go, this is your special trip. Can you forgive me?" she asked.

Luke was silent, *dumbstruck* even. That wasn't at all what he expected her to say. Kate never backtracked. She was always so sure of herself, and this, well, this wasn't at all like her. Her self-assured nature and strong self-confidence attracted him to her in the first place. Well, that, and her gorgeous green eyes and raven black hair. She rarely apologized. In fact, he couldn't remember her ever apologizing for anything before.

"Luke, are you going to say something?"

Luke wasn't one to speak, just to fill the silence. Still, he had to say something. But what? He had thought about their argument a lot last night, and he already knew in his heart what he was going to do. He just hadn't thought far enough ahead about how to say it. So this caught him flat-footed and, well, dumbstruck. But he cleared his throat and stammered a bit, "Um... well, thanks Kate, but you don't have to apologize. I'm the one who should apologize."

"No, Luke, wait..."

"Katie, please let me finish," Luke interrupted. And she did, because that wasn't like *him* at all. "You're my girl, and I love you. I don't want to be away from you on Thanksgiving. I think it's because I've been going on this hunting trip for so many years now, that it seemed like what I was supposed to do, so I argued for it. But the truth is, and I didn't even really know until last night, but what I really want is to be with you, more than anything else. When I thought it through, I know I would have a lousy time being away from you. It just wouldn't be Thanksgiving without you. My life's different now, Katie... Better. So, I guess what I'm trying to say is, I'm sorry, and I'd love to spend Thanksgiving with you and your folks."

Now it was Kate's turn to be silent, but Luke could hear her sniffling on the other end of the phone.

Oh no, what had he said wrong this time? *Oh brother,* Luke thought.

Then, after a few moments, Kate said, "I love you so much, Luke. I couldn't sleep at all last night, and this storm made it impossible. I've been tossing and turning all night, thinking about you, until I couldn't stand it for another minute. That's when I called you."

Luke was so caught up in the moment with Kate that he'd forgotten about the plane crash, the dark house, and even Archie laying on the floor next to him, as he stood there in the dark hallway.

"So it's settled then?" Luke asked. "We're spending Thanksgiving together with your folks?"

"Yes, yes, yes! Luke. Can I drive over this morning and make you breakfast? I really want to see you," Kate said excitedly.

"That would be great. I really want to see you too. Oh crap, Kate, I forgot to tell you. There was a plane crash over near the Country Club earlier tonight, and they've asked everyone to stay off the roads and stay indoors until they get things sorted out. I guess it was pretty bad. It was a big passenger jet, I think."

"What? Luke, why didn't you say anything? That's awful!"

"Well, I guess I was sort of surprised by your call, and then we started talking about us, and Thanksgiving, and I just forgot about it for a few minutes. I wanted to call you too, but was, well, I guess I was too afraid to or something, plus, it was so early in the morning that I thought you'd still be sleeping. I didn't sleep at all last night either."

"Luke, you said your power is out. How did you find out about it?"

"It was on when I first woke up. I was thinking about getting up and working on my book, since I couldn't sleep. Then, Jonah called and said he'd been trying to get ahold of me for a while, but the call wouldn't go through. Anyway, he told me to turn on the news, and that's when I saw it. We talked about it for a bit, but then Jonah had to go. He got called into work earlier and Ted was asking him to take care of something. So, we hung up, and that's when the lights went out. Come to think of it, it was kind of creepy. I was still holding the phone in my hand and staring at the television screen, kind of hypnotized by it. And then the lights went off."

"Honey, that's so terrible. Do you know how bad things are? Were there any survivors?" Kate asked.

"It looked pretty bad. I mean, pretty much as bad as a plane crash could look. I didn't watch for very long, but there was a lot of fire, and there were a lot of emergency vehicles and first-responders on the scene." Luke hesitated for a moment. "But there was this one thing that really freaked me out, Kate. It was this woman passenger, well I think she was a passenger. She was being treated by the paramedics. She was all covered in blood and her clothes torn and burned. They had her strapped down, but she was fighting them. It seemed not to fit... the way she was struggling, I mean. It was like she was hissing at them or something. But what got me the most were her eyes. They looked like they were solid black. Maybe it was the camera or the weird lighting there with all that was going on... but they had the camera right on her face for a moment - and she seemed so unnatural,

13

almost inhuman. Jonah said there was one other survivor besides her so far, but he didn't say much about her except that she ran away from the scene and into the woods behind the Country Club. But that didn't seem right either. I mean, why would she do that?"

"Luke, I'm getting my tablet and see if I can find out more. I'll call you back once I find out what's going on. I can drive over once they say it's okay. Will you be alright?"

"Yeah, I'll be fine. I'm gonna go get out my old camp stove and make some coffee. I think my MacBook's charged up, so I'll try to work on my book for a while until the lights come back on. Hey, at least it's nice and spooky around here for working on my story, you know, writing by candlelight with the wind howling outside. Katie, I'm glad we're okay. I miss you."

"Me too. I can't wait to see you. Oh, I have a surprise for you when I see you," Kate said with a sly grin.

"What?" Luke asked. "You can't leave it like that!"

"You'll just have to wait and see," she said.

"Hey, don't you have classes today?" Luke asked.

Kate was working on her Doctor of Education (ED.D.). at the University of Northern Iowa, which was in Waterloo, between Cedar Falls, where she still lived with her parents, and Luke's house, which was in Mason City.

"I have one class today, but I'm working on a big research project right now, and I really don't need to be on campus today. So, I can come see you instead," Kate said with a smile and a cheerfulness in her voice that also had Luke smiling. "Okay, Luke, go make your coffee, and I'll call you once I find out what's going on. Give Archie a scratch behind the ears and a big hug for me," Kate said.

"Love you," he said.

"Love you too."

They hung up, and Luke looked down at Archie, who was now standing, ears pointed straight up, listening intently, while staring ahead at the dark stairway. Just then, his hackles raised on his back and neck, and he growled low and deep.

Chapter 3

What's Out There

* * *

At seeing Archie like this, Luke froze and felt a sudden chill. He could feel his heartbeat harder in his chest while he tried to comprehend the moment. What was Archie so fixed on? He knew his pup, and Archie would only behave this way if something was there. Archie sensed something that didn't belong here. Was someone in the house with them? Then, a sort of scratching sound came from downstairs. Luke's heart beat faster still. He kept a handgun on his night table and he wondered if he should go get it. But something in his subconscious told him that if he did, then this would become real, and Luke didn't want it to be real, not in that way. *It must be a raccoon or something,* he thought. They had a lot of critters around here that were always getting into one thing or another. But then - Archie rarely growled at *them*.

"What is it, boy?" Luke whispered.

Archie only continued to growl, and his growl became more intense.

"Let's go see what it is," Luke tried to sound calm.

They started down the creaky stairs. Now the old house sounds were registering with Luke, and he cringed with each step. His phone was annoyingly dim after about 5 feet and cast a very broad and fading light as a candle might. Luke really wished he had recharged those flashlight batteries. His other two flashlights were downstairs in the kitchen and in the living room.

Bang! Bang! Bang!

Archie's growl became a vicious bark now, and Luke didn't think a raccoon could make *that* kind of noise. It was a loud bang against a window, almost as if someone, or *something*, were knocking hard against it. This *was* something real now. A bit of panic rose within Luke, and he decided that he really wanted his gun. He froze, and said in a whispered but firm tone, "Come on, Archie, let's go back upstairs." Luke turned to go back up the three steps they had moments ago descended, but Archie didn't follow. That wasn't like him at all. The banging wasn't letting up, and Luke didn't take the time to correct him. Though he hated to admit it, he felt better with Archie guarding the stairs while he ran back to the bedroom to get his gun.

Luke was moving in slow motion, as in a dream... He couldn't seem to get to his night table fast enough. Why did it seem so much farther than it was? After running through molasses, he made it to the night table, and he picked up his FNX-45, and then, in 10 giant running strides, he was back by Archie's side. Having the gun in his hand seemed to make him move faster, no more feeling as if his feet were glued to the floor. And it certainly made him feel better. It was a big handgun, with a 15-round magazine loaded with HST.45 rounds. Luke loved this gun, but he didn't get to practice with it as much as he wanted to.

As he got closer, he could tell that nothing had changed; the banging was even more persistent if anything and Archie was almost in a frenzy by the time Luke made it back to his side. He placed his hand on top of Archie's head and whispered, "It'll be okay Big Bear, Let's go take a closer look". Luke was glad that he had added a light onto his FNX, and he pressed the button with his left index finger to turn it on. The powerful beam lit up the entire stairway and glared off the large painting hanging on the wall at the bottom of the landing. The banging sound was erratic and loud, and as they descended the last few steps, Luke could now tell that it was coming from the front living room off the landing to the right of them. Archie, glued to Luke's side, moved in lock-step with him. The landing area was generous and had a large red and blue oval area rug that only covered half of the landing's hardwood floor. There was an old brass and crystal chandelier hanging over the rug that was equally grand, but dark and lifeless, without power. Luke paused at the last step before glancing left over the large curving maple handrail that led to the house's entryway foyer. To his right, the white paneled wall blocked the view of the front living room, from where the sound continued to rattle their nerves. The next step would allow Luke to see around the wall and into that room. Luke took the step, and the weapon light followed as he looked right. What Luke saw next made him gasp and involuntarily stumble backward. Even Archie whined and took a step back.

"Oh man, oh man, oh man! What the hell is that thing?" Luke cried out between panicked breaths. Luke trembled, and Archie was right there with him.

In the lower-left pane of the large 4-pane window closest to them, Luke saw what looked like his next-door neighbor, Mrs. Benson, with both of her hands, bloody and mangled, pounding in blood-smeared streaks on the thick double pane glass, and seemed oblivious that there were chunks of flesh missing from both, and what looked like strands of meat dangling from her palms and forearms. The bright light from his FNX showed it all in such clarity that there could be no mistaking what they saw before them. It was like a spotlight directly focused on Mrs. Benson's grotesque form. Then, Luke saw something he'd never forget as long as he'd live. Her face suddenly pressed firmly against the bloody, streaky window, and a gaping stringy hole where her throat should be was now in the spotlight, and her mouth was agape in a silent scream. Her eyes locked onto his in terror for a moment, and he could see the complete and utter pain she must be in, as her eyes and her endless stream of tears betrayed all that she was feeling in that moment. Luke heaved and rocked, and it took every ounce of his resolve not to puke all over the floor and on himself right then and there. Archie was still whimpering, but he took a step forward to stand next to Luke, who had already bent and put his hands on his knees in an attempt to hold back his bile, and also to keep the dizziness he felt from causing him to stumble further, and maybe even fall down. As he stood there, doubled over, for what seemed like minutes, the small part of his brain that was still aware of his surroundings, that *could* still be aware, registered that the banging had stopped, and all was silent now, except for the wind blowing through the trees outside. Luke slowly rose and took a few deep breaths to quell his nausea and fear. Archie was looking up at Luke with confusion and concern. Luke reached down and gently scratched the side of Archie's face. But he couldn't speak, for fear of tempting his nausea further. The gesture seemed to be enough, though, because Archie looked forward into the living room with his ears pricked once again, and his full attention was on the room in front of them.

Luke lifted his left hand again, the weapon light shining ahead, and the only thing out of place was the blood-streaked window. There was a lot of blood, but no more Mrs. Benson, no more banging. Nothing. Luke looked down at Archie and said, "I really don't wanna go anywhere near that window, boy." But he had too... Didn't he? What else could he do? But then, he thought of all those horror movies where you plead with the victim NOT to open *that* door... But she doesn't hear you, and opens it anyway. And it's always that singular mistake, that final idiotic act, that makes it - her last. That thought gave Luke pause. As much as he was being drawn to that window, he knew in his guts that he had to stay away from it. He would not be stupid. *Stupid gets you killed,* he thought. Where had that thought come from? Had he read or heard that somewhere?

Because it didn't feel like something he would say or think. His mind was racing, and his heart was pounding. He couldn't fathom what he was supposed to do next. What he saw wasn't real, it wasn't. It couldn't be. Could it? But there it was - right in front of him, 15 feet away, that bloody window. Then he thought of Kate, and he jammed his hand into his pocket to grab his phone, but it wasn't there. "Dammit, where is it?" he said. Then he remembered running to the bedroom to get his gun. *I must have left it there,* he thought. "C'mon, boy, let's go back upstairs to get my phone." Archie followed Luke without hesitation this time.

As they made their way to the curved staircase, his mind raced, and Luke thought about what he would say to Kate. What could he say? She'd never believe him. It was too unimaginable, and he didn't want to worry her. But whether she believed him or not, she would still worry about him. No, he decided, he wouldn't tell Kate. *Not yet.* They had just made up, and he wanted to hold on to that, for a while anyway. He would call Jonah instead. Jonah would know what to do. He knew Luke better than anyone else in the entire world, and he would know what to do.

When they reached the bedroom, Luke found the phone laying on the unmade bed with its light still on. Then he went to the window and stood off to the side, slid the long curtain a few inches, and tried to peek out through the small crack he made, but he couldn't see a damn thing. It was still so black outside. With the gentlest motion, Luke let the curtain go so that it didn't move too much, though he wasn't sure why he did that. The light from his gun was so bright that surely anyone outside that window would have seen it. Luke again took a deep breath, then made his way over to his bed and sat down on the edge. Archie hopped up and laid down next to Luke. He was visibly shaken. Luke began running his fingers through Archie's thick fur along his back and neck and could feel him trembling under his touch. "Pretty crazy, huh, boy? I'm scared to, but don't worry, I won't let anything happen to you," Luke tried to soothe Archie. His comforting words didn't lessen his own worry, though. *This is so messed up,* he thought.

Luke switched off the weapon light and reached for his phone laying next to his pillow, and touched the screen to make the call. He went to recent calls, then touched Jonah's call there. The phone rang several times, but Jonah didn't answer, and it went to his voicemail. Luke hung up, waited a minute, then called Jonah again. No answer. Luke tried a third time with growing frustration, but still no answer. He left Jonah a voicemail this time. "Hey man, please call me back as soon as you get this. Something really messed up has happened and I'm sort of freaking out here. Please call me back, bro." Luke touched the red phone button to end the call, and then opened the text messaging app. He typed out a similar message and pressed send. He stared at the screen for a while, waiting for a reply.

Luke placed his palm down on the bed with the phone still in it, thinking about what he should do. The phone vibrated under his palm and he flipped it over to see that it was Kate. Before he answered, he tried to decide between telling Kate or not telling Kate.

"Hey, Katie," Luke said. He tried to sound calm, but he could feel his voice trembling.

Kate didn't notice because she started rambling about what she found.

"Oh, Luke, oh I'm so glad you answered, baby. I'm seeing some pretty unbelievable stuff on the news and it's really freaking me out. Are you okay there?" Kate asked.

Luke hesitated, took a deep breath, let it out, and said, "I'm okay, but I'm a bit rattled over here myself. Something pretty unbelievable just happened, and I was trying to figure out what to do when you called. I thought about calling you, but I didn't want to worry you. I tried calling Jonah a moment ago, but he didn't pick up. "

"Luke, there are some really crazy attacks going on in several places. People are going insane and trying to bite anyone around them. I thought I was watching some sort of 'Blair Witch' faked reality thing - but it's on all the news channels, and being posted everywhere online. I saw one clip that looked like one woman was literally eating the face of another woman. Luke, her eyes were solid black. Then I remembered what you told me about the woman from the plane crash. I'm wondering if this is all a big hoax, but then why would the news be reporting it if it was? Honey, what's happening? I'm really scared! You said something was wrong there. What is it? Tell me what's happening, Luke."

"Oh crap, I just realized that I should probably call the police, Kate. For some reason, that never occurred to me until now. Can I call you right back?"

"No, wait, Luke, tell me what happened first, please," Kate said.

"Okay, well, it's like what you've been telling me. You know Mrs. Benson next door?" Luke asked.

"Yes, I remember her. She's that sweet widow lady you introduced me to a couple of months ago, kind of pretty older woman," Kate said.

"Yea, well, she's not so pretty anymore," Luke said. "She was just banging on my window downstairs, all bloody and torn. I don't even know how she was standing. Kate, there were *pieces* of her missing."

"Oh my god, Luke, that's exactly what I've been reading about, and seeing on the news. How can something like this really be happening? What did you do?" Kate asked.

"I didn't do anything. One minute she was there, and the next, she was gone. Just gone. I've never seen anything like that before, Kate. It was the worst thing I've ever seen. Shouldn't I call the police and report it? I know they'll probably think I'm nuts, but I should call them, right?"

"Please don't hang up yet, Luke. Stay on with me for a minute before you go. I'm afraid, and I don't want to let you go. Are you safe now?"

"I don't know, Kate. I really don't know. This just happened right before you called, but she's gone, and it's quiet now. I hope that's the last I see of her. We have to decide what we're going to do, Katie. I want to come to get you. Are your parents awake yet?" It was only. 4:00 AM, so Luke knew they were most likely still sleeping.

"No, but Papa usually wakes up at 5:00 AM every day. I think I will wake them up to tell them what is happening. Will you stay on with me while I go up to their room?" Kate asked.

Luke thought about how this was going to sound to her parents and decided that he'd better stay on with her in case she needed him.

"Of course I will," Luke said.

Archie jolted to a standing position on the bed and looked toward the bedroom door. Then, an instant later, a loud crash, followed by the tinkling of glass on the hardwood floor, came from downstairs.

Chapter 4

They're in Here

$* * *$

Luke jerked at the unexpected sound, as if shocked by an electrical current. His breath hitched into the phone, and Archie once again began his low growl, his posture rigid, and the fur on the back of his neck and back bristling. Kate sensed it as if she were next to him. She felt his shock through the phone.

"Luke, sweetheart, what's wrong?" she said, worried.

"Oh god Kate, oh god, something just broke through a downstairs window," Luke said in a panic.

Then, a slow dragging, shuffling sound, followed by, *Thump! Thump! Thump!* Something heavy was slowly coming up the stairs.

Luke had never in his life experienced genuine terror, and his mind and body reacted in a way that he didn't understand. He was shaking, and he felt a sudden surge of energized fear run through his very core. It felt as if he were gasping for every breath, and his heart was pounding in his chest and ears at an impossible rate. Luke stood, in a panic, and dropped the phone, unaware that he had done either. His body's built-in protective mechanism of fight or flight had taken

23

over, something he'd never experienced before. Luke was no longer thinking, but acting on pure instinct. He grabbed his handgun from the bed and moved with inhuman speed to the doorway, and pressed his back against the wall next to it, with his right shoulder touching the door frame, waiting for whomever, or whatever it was, to come into the room. It would not see him when it did.

Archie was still standing on the bed, rigid, his stance forward-leaning, as if being held by an invisible taught chain. He was barking as a rabid dog might, with long strands of drool hanging from his mouth. Luke and Archie were a sight, both instantly transformed by this gripping fear into two completely different beings. They were both ready to fight. But fight what?

As the thing continued up the stairs, in a slow, grueling climb, Luke was regaining control over his breathing. His mind was also clearing with each step of the thing, as if turning the lens of a telescope, to bring it more into focus. The thing's movement slowed further as it reached the top of the stairs and began shuffling down the hallway. As it neared the door, a soft, raspy, hissing sound billowed through the air. Archie jumped down from the bed, and in a crouch, prowled closer to the door. Luke looked at Archie for the first time since he heard the window shatter. Luke was only aware of two things at that moment; Archie was there with him, and that they shared a common purpose to protect each other and themselves from whatever was coming closer... closer.

Then the hissing stopped, and then the movement of the thing stopped. It was silent for a few moments. And then came a dragging sound, against the wall just outside the door.

A haunting and enormous face crept in around the doorjamb and appeared above Luke's head, looking down on him. Luke stumbled back in surprise, several steps, and shone his weapon light on the beast of a man. He was not expecting to look up and suddenly see the thing quietly towering over him, after all the racket that they had endured over the past few heart-pounding minutes. It was human, but... not human. Not anymore. It was grotesque, bloody, and torn, with its entire right jawbone and teeth exposed from a gaping hole in its cheek. Bloody? Maybe that wasn't the right word. It was more like a black sludge, and it was oozing out from his mangled flesh. A pungent smell followed, that even in Luke's current panicked state, made him gag. The thing had to have been well over 6'5", as his head was only inches from the top of the doorway. When the body of the thing followed its grotesque head and squeezed through the doorway in an almost slow-motion lunge toward Luke, it was the largest man that Luke had ever seen in person. He was massive, and had to be over 350 pounds of blubber, and flesh, and bones. The clothes he wore, if they could still be called that, were like rags now, hanging from him. His white dress shirt was in ribbons as it hung from its massive shoulders, a necktie still attached in mocking irony. The white, shredded undershirt it had on was no longer white at all, with rolls of fat from the thing hanging out, jiggling, and oozing the black vicious fluid where chunks of flesh were missing, with every movement it made. The thing opened its mouth, and let out a god-awful gurgling sound that told Luke all he needed to know. Luke, desperate, already had his gun pointed at the beast of a *man,* and he squeezed the trigger, but nothing happened. "Oh god please, no!" Luke squeaked out. He tried yet again and it still wouldn't fire, but then he realized he had forgotten to chamber a round and to switch off the safety. Frantically, he racked the slide on the FNX, dropped the safety with his left thumb, and pulled the trigger several times. The sound of the .45 caliber pistol firing in the small room was deafening. Ears ringing, Luke had to dive out of the way as the gargantuan thing toppled towards him. The entire room shook as it hit the floor. Dresser-top items and pictures on the walls rattled and clinked under the shockwaves of the thing, crashing down hard. Luke scrambled to Archie's side, who had stopped his frenzied barking, with his gun and light still pointed at the creature. Luke felt an overwhelming sense of relief at seeing the stinking, rotting thing lying on the floor, motionless. But the putrid odor of the creature was even more overpowering now, and it made Luke's eyes water, even over the smell of spent gunpowder lingering in the room. He reached down to touch Archie's head as he stood next to him. But his companion began to bristle and growl again. The damn thing moved, slowly at first, but within a few seconds, it was attempting to stand once again.

Luke was confused by the site, and could not comprehend how this *man* could still move after he had shot it at point blank range several times. "No, no, no!" he yelled. "You can't!"

Archie didn't hold back any longer. Mouth frothing, and body charged with adrenaline, he launched his 90 pounds of muscle, and teeth, and fur, and rage at the hideous, once man *thing*, and began tearing into his arms and shoulders wherever his 250 pounds of biting force could gain purchase, as the rotting, stinking thing tried to push itself up from the floor. German Shepherds are known for their protective nature, agility, and powerful bite, and Archie's abilities were on full display as he unleashed his unbridled fury on the man-thing. Chunks were being ripped and pulled from the rotting thing in a blur, as black syrupy ooze was pouring from every place that Archie could rip meat and muscle from bone. Luke was in awe of the site because he had never seen Archie attack anything before, and didn't really know how incredibly powerful and vicious he could be when provoked. Archie was like an unstoppable, wild, snapping demon. The sight gave Luke goosebumps. He stared at his loving companion as he transformed into a vicious fighting machine, protecting his master from this unknown and horrifying threat. It was working; as the foul-smelling creature attempted several times to regain footing, and an equal number of times it was put down and overwhelmed by the savage yet skillful fighter that Archie had become. But as the number of attempts grew, Luke could see that Archie was getting fatigued. He would sometimes stop for long moments, breathing hard and resting over his prey, in a posture of dominance, but losing energy fast. The stinking creature lay face down and motionless on the floor. But on the creature's final try, when it seemed that the disgusting and mangled thing was finished, that he, *it*, surprised Archie with a sudden burst of speed, for such a large and lumbering thing, and reached behind itself and grabbed Archie by the scruff of his neck. It then threw Archie with such unexpected force that he flew across the room, and violently hit one of the old bed's large hardwood posts, falling motionless on the floor.

"Archie! No!" Luke flew to his companion's side, slid to a stop, and dropped to the floor next to him. Tears began streaming down Luke's cheeks as he softly caressed the side of Archie's face and searched desperately for any sign of life from his beautiful Shepherd. Devastated, Luke lost all awareness of everything around him, except for his pup lying on the floor in a heap, lifeless. But something distant in his mind was screaming at him, trying to remind him of the imminent danger in the room, but it wasn't strong enough to pull Luke away as he gently attempted to revive his Archie. As he stroked Archie's face, with tears streaming down his own, he was heartbroken. It was a pain like he'd never felt before. He loved his dog beyond words, and the gut-wrenching pain pulled sobs from deep within Luke and racked his breathing. Luke couldn't fathom what had just happened; one minute he and Archie were running on full charge, and together in a fight for survival, side-by-side, master and companion. And the next, his Archie lay lifeless on the floor. It happened in an instant.

Luke felt the floor vibrate beneath him, and there was a sort of faint gurgling sound far off in the distance. As he felt the vibrations getting stronger, the sound growing louder, more immediate, Luke felt himself being pulled back into the room with the man... thing, whatever it was, with its gagging stench and nightmarish features. Understanding slowly came back into focus for Luke, of his situation, his very dire situation. Then, Luke's pain changed, turned into something else, but equally as intense. It was another emotion that Luke had never felt before, and it was driving him with a force he could not control. He wanted, no, needed, to kill that thing that had just taken his Archie away from him.

As he palmed the pistol that was lying on the floor next to him, and positioned it in his hand so that he could use it on the monster,

Luke turned to his side to face the thing, when suddenly he felt a dizzying blow, and then a massive pressure pushing him into the floor. There was darkness, and he could scarcely breathe, and his hand was now trapped beneath him, still holding the pistol, crushing his hand. Luke could not move, he could not breathe, he could not make a sound. But he could smell, and this cold and rotting thing that was pressing him down with its massive weight was dripping its black, stinking ooze all over him. He was so engulfed by the horrid stench that he could taste it. Luke screamed, he screamed like he had never screamed before, but there was hardly a sound. And as he screamed, he pushed with every ounce of his being to move from under this thing, before it... Before it, what? What did it want Luke for? Luke realized he didn't know, but he knew that if he didn't somehow get out from under this dead, smelling thing, that he would soon be dead himself. He was suffocating. He needed air, but could hardly pull in enough to sustain himself. As he pushed, and pushed, he felt he was finally gaining some leverage and able to lift an inch, and then an inch more, and could almost move his hand holding his gun. Almost. Luke pushed again, and again, and somehow turned one of his legs sideways, and brought his knee up just far enough to give him the leverage he needed to push the thing up a fraction of an inch more. It was enough to pull his hand from underneath him. When he did, he pushed the FNX into its side, and pulled the trigger again and again. He didn't know how many times, 5, 10; he didn't know. The stinking thing writhed and moaned, and moved just enough off of Luke for Luke to pull his head free from under the thing, turn it to the side and gasp for air, and then the pistol fell from his numb hand. He sucked in air as if he had been drowning. But it was in that instant that Luke knew exactly what it wanted. He saw the thing's black eyes and open, rotting mouth descending upon his face. *The eyes, the same black eyes...* Then, Luke knew. He somehow knew that all of this had something to do with that plane crash, but it was too late. It was so close now that Luke could see the blackness within its mouth, and the faint light in the room from his weapon light, glowing through the hole in the rotting things's missing cheek. It was inhuman and cold, but it was hungry, and all Luke saw was the mouth of the creature growing larger, closer, with rotting chunks of something between its teeth, and there was no escape. Luke knew he was going to die. Tears streamed from his eyes again in a flood, and he whimpered out two words; "God, please..." He squeezed his eyes shut, hoping it would somehow hurt less if he didn't see it.

There was a long pause, then the thing was suddenly moving violently, and Luke said a silent prayer as he tried to close his eyes even tighter. He could do little else. He heard a sickening crunch, and a gush of the black sludge fell on Luke's face and neck, and he waited for the pain to register. But he felt nothing. Is that what it was supposed to be like? No feeling or pain at all? Then, unexpectedly, the hideous thing stopped moving, dropping in a dead weight back down on top of Luke. He felt that! He slowly opened his eyes. What was happening? Had the thing bitten him and was now taking a break before the next bite? Luke still felt nothing, though, other than the massive weight on top of him, crushing him. At least Luke's head and left arm were still out from under the thing. He moved his left hand up to his face and felt the greasy stinking ooze, and he frantically wiped it away with his one free hand, feeling and searching for the missing part of his own face. But it was all there, and there was nothing wrong with him. *What had just happened?* Luke thought. He was definitely still alive, because he could still feel this unbearable weight on top of him and he could scarcely breathe. Luke had to get out from under it. He had to do something - and do it now!

Then a sound, a rhythmic sniffing sound, followed by a soft whining that Luke recognized instantly.

Chapter 5

Archie

* * *

"Archie!" Luke croaked out, almost inaudible, "I'm over here." He could just make out from the corner of his eye, his beautiful Archie beginning to come into focus. But Luke was in such an awkward position, trapped under this putrid mass, face down, with only his head and left arm poking out from under one side of the thing. He was at least able to place his face sideways with his cheek against the floor. He had no more strength to push the thing off or to wiggle his way out from under it. Though spent, Luke beamed at his Shepherd, coming closer to him. When Archie found Luke's face poking out, he began whining with happiness, nuzzling Luke's ear and neck with his long, fuzzy snout and warm nose. Luke was having a hard enough time breathing already, without that, but he didn't care. He was so glad to see his pup alive, and his heart was bursting with joy and relief. Luke tried to say more, but he couldn't speak, for the force pressing down on him.

From deep within, Luke summoned a tiny surge of strength at seeing his Archie, and he pushed and shoved with all his might. The dead heap only moved a fraction of an inch, but it did move! Archie then understood what his master was trying to do, and jumped to the other side and grabbed the rotting arm of the creature and bit down hard, then he pulled with every fiber of his 90 pounds. Archie was a strong Shepherd, almost all muscle and agility, and Luke felt it instantly, and pushed harder and harder from his awkward position. Luke had almost no leverage, but, painfully, and a fraction of an inch at a time, his shoulders and other arm, and part of his chest, were free of the disgusting blubbery thing. Almost there, but he had to get his legs free. Luke pulled with every ounce of strength he had left to free them, and from the other side, Archie pulled on the foul and rotting man, and together, with one last effort, Luke was free!

Exhausted, panting for air, and face pouring sweat, Luke barely had the strength to whisper, "Thank you Lord." Archie hopped back over to Luke's side, and though weary himself, couldn't control his need to pounce all around Luke, giving him kisses, and nuzzling him all around his face and shoulders. Luke, tears streaming down his cheeks, knowing that they were both okay, but he had to push Archie away from his face, because he knew that thing's blood, or whatever it was, still covered him. "Hey boy, I'm glad to see you, too. Thanks for helping me out there. I really thought it had me for a few minutes there. How are you Big Bear? I thought you were a goner, too." Luke scratched him behind his ears and rubbed his face with both hands.

Luke wondered how things had changed so quickly. He was certain that the thing was about a half second away from taking a big bite right out of his face. He looked over at the lifeless beast laying there on its stomach. Then he looked at Archie, and he stood up on wobbly legs. He took a half step closer, almost expecting the thing to jump back up and come at him again. But Archie was not on guard in that way, as if he knew the thing was truly dead. Luke took one more pensive step, and as he stood over it, he noticed just below its greasy head that the entire back of his neck was missing. A sizable chunk was missing right out of its spine below the head. Luke looked back down at Archie. "You do that?" Archie looked back up at him with his big baloney tongue hanging out of the side of his mouth, with a playful look in his eyes. Luke shook his head in wonder at Archie and ruffled the top of his head. "You saved us, boy, you know that, right?"

Bark!

"What the hell is happening?" Luke never swore, and it was very unlike him. He grew up in a household where you never heard a curse word or an angry voice. His mom and dad were both very strong in their own way, but they were kind and decent folks, and they were a very loving Christian family. But this was really messed up, and Luke didn't think any of this was even possible. But there it was, right in front of him, something, a man, well, it was once a man, anyway. Now it was something else. What, though? And this nightmare event was bringing out an angry side within him he didn't realize he had. He remembered the lady on the news, her eyes, the way she seemed to fight against the paramedics. He remembered Mrs. Benson through his living room window. Then, this thing on the floor in front of him. They all had the same eyes, and they all were impossibly alive when they should have been dead. Were they dead? *That's crazy,* he thought. Luke really wanted to check the news, but without power... Then he remembered his phone. "Crap, my phone! Katie!" In a panic, he searched for his phone. What had he done with it? He remembered he was talking with Kate when the window shattered downstairs. But then what? "Did I drop it on the floor somewhere?" Luke shone his weapon light on the floor all around, looking in every corner, on the bed, under the bed, and then, there it was, halfway under the dresser. Luke reached down and picked it up, knowing that it was too much to hope that Katie was still on the other end waiting for him. He looked at the screen. Nothing! It was black and lifeless. He began pushing buttons. Still nothing. He pressed the power button and held it down, then an image of a battery highlighted in red appeared on the screen. "No, no, no, no!"

"Now what Archie? We have no power, no phone, and now this thing laying on our bedroom floor." Then he realized he was also thirsty. He knew Archie must be near dehydration, too. "Okay, first things first boy, let's go get some water."

Bark, Bark!

Archie knew the word water, and he left no doubt that he wanted some, too.

Luke stuck his dead phone in his sweatpants back pocket and started for the bedroom door to head downstairs to get some cold water from the kitchen. It was such a normal thing to do, and they had done it a thousand times before without even thinking about it. But as they neared the stairway to head downstairs, Luke stopped, looked down at Archie, and realized this wasn't a normal thing at all, not now. He took a deep breath and realized he didn't know what to do. After a few moments, he turned back to go to the large bathroom down the hall. This time, Archie stayed glued to Luke's side.

In this old Victorian house, there were no bathrooms in the bedrooms, like there were in newer homes. All the bathrooms were shared, and off the hallways. It was early morning, but it was still very dark outside, so Luke still used his weapon light to see. When they made it into the bathroom, Luke flipped the light switch out of habit, and then gave a forced half smile and shook his head at his mistake. He looked around the bathroom for something to put water in for Archie, but couldn't find anything large enough. Luke couldn't use the tub, because the side was too high for Archie to lean over and drink from it, unless he filled it all the way to the top. Then he looked at the toilet. "No, we're not that desperate yet, boy." He settled on the sink and using his hands. Putting his gun down on the counter next to him, he turned the handle on the cold water faucet. Luke must have cupped his hands and filled them at least twenty times to give Archie enough water to satisfy him. Archie gulped every handful as if he hadn't had a drink in days. After several minutes of this process, when Archie had his fill, he turned his head away and lay down on the floor next to Luke's feet. Luke didn't mind waiting. He always put Archie first, even after the long runs they would take on most days together. He thought of the Old West, and the cowboys taking care of their horses before themselves. Well, at least that's what the good ones did in the movies, anyway. He didn't bother filling the tiny cup that was sitting next to the sink. Instead, he leaned over and put his lips to the stream of cold water coming right out of the faucet. It felt to Luke like he was standing there, drinking, for 5 minutes straight. He was so very thirsty. Finally, belly full, and thirst quenched, he splashed some water on his face and grabbed the bar of soap sitting in a small dish next to the sink. He scrubbed his face, ears, neck, hands, and anywhere he could get to without taking a shower, the best he could. That was one nasty stinking creature, and the stink was still all over him. When Luke was done, he grabbed a towel and dried his face, neck, and hair. He saw a t-shirt hanging out of the clothes bin next to the door, and he reached down and grabbed it. "Anything is better than this," he said, as he pinched the one he was wearing, and pulled it away from his chest and then let it go. He gingerly pulled it over his head, so as not to get more of the crap that was all over it on his clean face. "Man, I should have taken this thing off first." Archie looked up at Luke, still laying on the floor. He pulled the dirty one from the hamper over his head and felt a lot better. He thought of the Old West again and wondered if that's what they did back then, too.

Now what? He thought. Then, he remembered his dad's saying again about a man being strong, and making up his mind about a thing and sticking to it. Luke decided he had to do something and hoped it would be the right thing. He thought about that monstrosity crashing through the living room window and realized there was now a broken window downstairs. With little effort at all, anything could come through that window now. And then he thought that even the other windows weren't much use either. Not from those things, anyway.

"We aren't safe here, Archie." And Luke knew then that keeping them safe was the most important thing to do. But how?

He turned off his weapon light and used the very faint glow coming from the candlelight still burning down the hall in his bedroom. He did this for two reasons: First, to avoid drawing

34

anymore attention to the house, or to him and Archie. *Was it already too late?* He only wished that he'd thought of that sooner. The second reason was to save the battery in the light for a time when they might need it more. The light on the FNX was powerful, and the battery was small, so it couldn't last *forever*. He had to be careful not to use it unless he needed it. He thought about all that had happened, and decided that so far, they had really needed it.

"Archie, come boy," he whispered to his resting pup. He wanted to make his way downstairs to his study to get his shotgun from the gun safe, and to get some more ammunition for his FNX. Luke had grown up hunting with his Gramps and father, so having a gun or two in the house was just something they always did. But Luke's dad had been very strict about gun safety, so they had always kept them in a gun safe. Over the past couple of years, though, Luke bent that rule and started keeping a gun on his night table while he was sleeping. He was sure glad he had it in his hand now.

When they reached the top landing, he stood still for a few moments and listened. There was no sound except for the howling wind outside, which he knew could mask a million other sounds. But Archie seemed relaxed, so he figured they were safe for now. Luke took the first tentative step on the stairway, dreading the creaking sound that he knew would follow, then the second, and then the third. He stopped again and listened. Other than the wind, all was still quiet. They took two more steps, then he heard a scream through the wind outside. It was faint, but wrought with pain and terror. There was no mistaking what it was. Archie's ears went straight up, and he was rigid and alert again. The fear was once again building within Luke and was gripping him like a vise. He didn't want to face another one of those things. His heart pounded hard and he could feel the adrenaline once again course through him. Luke had made up his mind to get to that gun safe, and that's what they were going to do. Three more steps, and they stopped and listened again. It was almost perfectly black near the bottom landing. No light from the candle in his bedroom upstairs filtered down this far, and Luke couldn't see a thing. He was moving by memory and touch. He knew this house, though, and could picture every detail as he descended the final few stairs. They needed to move only a few more steps and then left toward the entryway. Luke's study was only a few feet down a short hallway past there, and he could navigate that with his eyes closed. *I hope the broken window is in the living room.* He thought it was because that's where he saw Mrs. Benson, and it sounded like the wind was louder coming from that side. But there were two large windows in the entryway too, and that's the direction Luke and Archie needed to go.

Luke patted Archie's face with the palm of his right hand. "Okay, boy, let's keep going."

All was still and quiet. Luke took the last step and was now on the bottom landing, and he could feel Archie staying tight against his right leg. He listened intently and put his hand on Archie's head. Archie knew to stay right by his master's side, and he made no sound, somehow knowing they needed to be silent. Luke curled around the staircase banister on his left and kept his back tightly against it as he moved closer to the wall it was connected to. He knew he was nearing the antique mahogany table that was against that wall, so he put his hand out to gently feel for it. As his fingertips found the table, a flash of lightning filled the large entryway windows, and in that half-second of flickering light, the horror that stared back at Luke through those large windows made him swoon.

Chapter 6

Run!

* * *

Looking back through the windows were at least a half dozen bloody and torn faces, just like Mrs. Benson's. When the flash of lightning illuminated their ghastly forms, they seemed to look directly at Luke, as if they knew he would stand in that very spot at that exact moment. In an instant they were there, grotesque and impossibly still alive, and the next, they were gone, hidden away once again by the darkness. But they already seared into Luke's eyes, and he knew they were there, though he could no longer see them. And they were there *for him!* But why? How?

Luke's heart was again pounding in his chest, and he began to hyperventilate, and he could not regain control over his breathing. His body was taking over in ways that were completely foreign to him. In the deepest recesses of his mind, he could hear his own voice screaming at him to *RUN!* But his body would not obey. His hands went to his knees, and he almost tripped over Archie, who was standing still and quiet next to him. Luke tried to suck in a deep breath to slow his involuntary gasping, but he couldn't command his body at all; it just would not listen. He was vaguely aware of Archie beginning to bark now, but it was distant and dreamlike. Then, breaking glass, gurgling sounds, and inhuman moans filled the air all at once. Luke had to move, and he had to move now. He knew it, and somehow the urgency and the adrenaline flooding his bloodstream pushed him to act. Luke screeched in a voice that he himself didn't recognize, "Archie, run!"

The moment Luke turned to run, his left foot hooked the table leg, and he tripped over it and went sprawling face first across the hardwood floor. The awkward fall jarred the FNX from his hand and he could hear it slide further down the hall and clatter against something as it came to a stop. His palms and knees were stinging from the sudden hard fall to the floor. That seemed to be what Luke needed to awaken his full awareness of the situation, because he realized he needed to find an escape from these things and he knew he only had seconds to do it. But where?

"Archie, come!" he commanded in the most urgent voice he could muster. Archie flew to his side and Luke felt him slam against his leg, and then they ran in the opposite direction from where the crazy, bloody people were coming from. The sounds of thumping and hissing were so close, but he could not see them. He couldn't see anything. Luke knew this old house, every doorway, every turn, every angle, but the terror he was feeling was overpowering and it was clouding his ability to think. He felt for the large entryway into the sitting room and made the turn once he felt the hardwood beam that marked its opening. Then, a loud yelp came from his side, and he didn't feel Archie next to him anymore. "Archie!" Luke screamed. Then, savage sounds filled the air mere feet from him, but in complete darkness. Luke's heart was breaking for Archie because he couldn't see him, couldn't help him. "Archie, hang on boy, I'm coming. Fight! Fight!" Luke yelled. And he heard him, and all of his fury, in his terrible fight for survival once again. Luke dropped to the floor and began wildly scrambling to find his pistol. It was the only thing he could think of to do. But was it here or in the hallway? He didn't know, but he knew he needed that light, needed that gun. He rammed his fingers into every nook, against every piece of furniture, sliding across the floor on his hands and knees frantically feeling, searching, in complete and utter darkness.

Archie continued to fight and snarl, and the hissing thing, or things, were just as vicious and loud. Luke had to help him. He had to find that gun. He knew he was helpless until he did. Every second felt like minutes, and Luke could feel Archie's pain and fear. Archie's snarls, barks, and yelps were gripping Luke's very soul. Man, how he loved that dog. He was aching for his pup, and with every fiber of his being, he needed to help him. Another yelp of pain from Archie, and this one squeezed Luke's heart like a vise. In one of Luke's wild sweeps of his hands across the floor, the outer edge of his right hand banged hard against the ornate and curved leg of one of the old Victorian couches in the sitting room they were in. The sting of pain was sharp and numbing. Then deeper under the couch, his hand slid, and there, his fingertips felt the rough diamond cut grip of the FNX. He stretched further and further until he could wrap his hand around it, and then he finally grasped it and pulled it out.

Archie, still snarling and savagely defending himself, to Luke, sounded further away now. Luke moved the gun to his left hand and pressed the weapon light's side button, and it instantly illuminated the room with a blinding white light. Luke spotted one of the things laying on the floor awkwardly, with its head and neck bent at an unnatural 90-degree angle from its shoulders, with a gooey black hole where its throat should have been. It looked like it might have been a teenage girl, and it was motionless. Luke heard Archie's rumbling, deep growl, but he wasn't in the room. Luke ran for the entryway to the sitting room and into the large wood-paneled hallway, and there, he saw Archie in a crouch about to leap at the woman, or thing, in front of him. She was a large woman with long greasy black hair. She had the same black eyes as the others, and one of her arms was just... gone. Strings of what Luke guessed were veins and tendons or muscle were dangling below the shoulder, but the woman didn't seem to care. Gaping rips and tears riddled the flesh of her thighs and calves, soaking her pink sweatpants in an oily black ooze. Had Archie done that? Luke didn't know, but his dog was preparing to strike again at the hissing woman, whom Luke could now see was also missing her right ear. There was a big black hole in the side of her face where it should be, and black liquid was leaking out of it and down her cheek and onto her white and blue Kansas City Royals jersey.

Luke didn't wait for Archie to attack her again. He lifted his gun and gripped it tightly with his right hand wrapped under and around his left. He aimed at the woman and squeezed the trigger twice. The explosions of the two large .45 caliber rounds firing were deafening. Luke's ears were ringing, and Archie jumped and moved back a step. The woman didn't go down! Knocked backwards and staggering, she maintained her footing and looked at Luke with an almost puzzled look. Then she opened her mouth wide and hissed at him, and moved towards him. Her dead black eyes locked onto his. Luke aimed again, but this time he aimed for her head. He squeezed the trigger, and her head snapped back violently before she dropped to the floor. Luke turned to look for Archie, who was still in a defensive stance, ready to fight if needed. Luke wanted so much to grab Archie up in a big bear hug and look him over for injuries, but he knew they had to move before more of those things found them. They were not safe here, and Luke knew they couldn't keep fighting like this in the dark and hope to survive. They'd been lucky twice now, and Luke was sure their luck was running out. But where? How? They were inside the house now. Luke thought of the Attic, but there was no way he and Archie could get up there. It was all the way upstairs, and they would have to pass by the front part of the house again, and that's where the hideous creatures were coming in. Besides, how would he get Archie up there? Luke was strong, but he doubted he could get Archie up those steep ladder steps by himself. Not in the dark, and not in the few moments they had left before more of those people found them. Then Luke thought of the basement. Grandpa had turned that into a bomb shelter, back in the 50s, and though Luke hadn't been down there in, he didn't know how long. The basement door was in the back of the house, a few feet off the mudroom.

Luke heard the crunching of broking glass and knew that more of them were inside now. He decided he needed speed, and that was more important than turning the light off. Besides, those things found him and Archie in the pitch darkness and attacked Archie, so did it really even matter?

"Let's go, boy!" Luke said as panic filled him again. They ran out of the sitting room and back into the large hallway and then turned to run toward the back of the house where the mudroom and basement door were located. The rancid smell of these hideous and savage things was heavy in the air, and Luke couldn't remember ever smelling something so awful before. He gagged with every breath. The scratching and thudding sounds were growing louder behind them as they made it into the large kitchen. Luke slid to a stop at the breakfast table, and then they bounded to the left, where the mudroom was. The heavy metal door that led down to the basement was just to the right of the mudroom.

When he heard the things crashing into the table and chairs in the kitchen, he knew they were out of time. He grabbed the lever style handle of the basement door and pushed down to open it, but the door wouldn't budge! Archie bristled and barked viciously again; he was ready to attack, and Luke could feel the surrounding air change as the lumbering people, or monsters, or whatever they were, were now only 15 feet away. There were three of them, and as they approached Luke and Archie in their slow and unnatural herky-jerky movements. Luke couldn't help but stare for a moment in panic and awe. A moment they did not have to spare. The disgusting forms almost seemed to move by invisible strings that he knew couldn't be there. This grotesque trio looked as if they were some sort of night-marish family. There was a man, a woman, and a young boy, perhaps 13, and they were all in various states of broken, torn, and bloody. Luke gagged and felt the bile coming up to his mouth when he looked at the man's middle, and only his fear kept him from losing control of his stomach's contents. There was a gaping black hole there, and disgusting strands of something torn and stringy were hanging out of him. Luke could not comprehend why or how these people were even moving, or what had happened to them.

They lurched and shuffled, in a sickening sort of rhythm and time with one another, with a single-mindedness of getting to Luke and Archie. Luke grabbed the doorknob once more and rattled it in a panic, but it would still not move. His only other choice was to go outside through the solid maple door of the mudroom, but he was terrified of what he might run into if he opened that door. No, better to face what he knew, and could see, than to go out there. Ten feet away, and Archie was now simultaneously barking, snapping, and drooling like a rabid dog. Luke raised his FNX with his shaky hands and he did his best to aim at the head of the biggest of the three, the man, and he pulled the trigger.

BOOM!

The thing's head exploded, vanishing in a mist as the large-caliber round made impact. Only a small chunk of it remained as it dangled from the man's neck. Then the entire mass of the man dropped to the floor with a sickening wet thud into a puddle of the disgusting black ooze that had formed at its feet.

Seven feet now, and the two remaining shuffling dead things didn't even flinch at the sound of the exploding round. He aimed again, this time at the woman. Her dead black eyes locked onto Luke in a lifeless stare, a hissing sound emitting from her throat, through a mouth that was opened in a painful snarl. Luke squeezed the trigger, but nothing happened. The trigger wouldn't even move. He tried again and again frantically, but the slide had locked back, the chamber empty. Luke glanced down at it and saw what he just didn't want to believe. He was out of bullets.

The woman raised her arms in a ghoulish jerking motion, as she was now only two steps away, and Luke could now see that one of her hands was missing, and only mangled strands of flesh hung from the wrist where her hand should have been. Luke saw she was wearing a skimpy nightgown, and couldn't help thinking that she must have been quite beautiful before. *Before what?* The putrid gagging smell wafted to his nostrils and his eyes watered from the overwhelming stench coming off her. And that last thought disappeared as fast as it came. Luke would not let this nasty rotting woman touch him, so he leaned back on his left leg, which was slightly behind him, from trying to fire his FNX at the thing just before, and he kicked out hard with his right leg and drove his foot into the woman's chest, causing her to stumble hard backwards and fall to the floor.

The boy was now also in reach, and *he* lunged for Luke, but Archie did not hold back any longer. He threw his 90 pounds at the boy in a predatory and blinding fury. Archie was easily as large as the boy, and probably weighed even more, and the boy was no match for the agile and muscular Shepherd. Archie ripped and tore at every place he could grip with his powerful jaws, as the boy flailed around on the floor in an absurd jerky slow-motion dance in an attempt to get Archie off him. The boy writhed and gurgled in a sickening scramble as he threw his head back and arched his back in a wild attempt to escape Archie's snapping jaws, but in doing so, exposed and presented his throat to Archie. It was the last movement the boy ever made. Instinctively, Archie wrapped his massive jaws around the offering and bit down hard, crushing the throat and spine of the creature in a sickening, juicy crunch.

Luke was looking around for something to fend off the woman, beginning to push herself up from the floor, and grabbed the coat stand from the mudroom. It was large and unwieldy, so he had to set his FNX down to maneuver it with both hands. He put the gun down on a small shelf on the wall and tried to aim the light in the woman's direction, because it was their only source of light. Luke did not want to be in the dark again, and hoped that the light would hold out until he could find his flashlight, or the lights came back on.

Before Luke could advance with his large awkward coat rack in hand, he saw Archie leap from the motionless boy toward the woman. As Archie landed at the woman's feet, he seized her calf in his jaws, bit down hard, and began convulsing and shaking his head as he ripped and pulled. He seemed to understand that removing her balance would cause her to fall back to the floor, and she did. She toppled over in an undignified and clumsy manner, just as Luke had closed the distance with his coat rack. With one giant arching swing over his head, as if he were going to split a giant log with an axe, he brought the coat rack down hard onto the woman's face. Like so much bad jam, the black sludgy ooze pooled around her squashed head, and she, too, was now motionless. Luke lifted the heavy coat rack over his head again, and brought it down on her a second time, to be certain. The resulting mess, *and smell*, was not pretty.

Archie looked up at his master with his tongue hanging out, and he seemed to smile. It was like when they played together and Archie was happy. "Are you pleased with yourself, boy?" Luke ruffled the top of Archie's head, and then heard more glass breaking in the front of the house.

"Crap, not again! Let's get this door open, Big Bear."

Chapter 7

Nowhere to Hide

* * *

Luke made his way back to the shelf to grab his gun and thought what an expensive flashlight it had become. But he was so very thankful for it. It was like a lifeline that he did *not* want to lose. He did not know what time it was, but it was still very dark outside, and there was no light coming from any of the windows near to them. He went back to the basement door and stood there for a moment and jiggled the lever-style handle again. Luke didn't want to face anymore of those things, and he had nothing to protect them with. But then he looked down at Archie and rubbed the top of his head affectionately. "I've got you, boy." Luke heard sirens far off in the distance and felt a small sense of relief. *At least there's some help out there,* he thought.

His mind began moving in ten different directions at once, as he tried to understand what was happening. His small world had been turned into a living nightmare right inside his own house, but he hadn't yet given any thought to what was happening out there in the rest of the world. He had been a little preoccupied with their own survival. How were his neighbors and friends doing? He couldn't be the only one this was happening to. He knew that much. Then he remembered the screams that he'd heard earlier, and he wondered if those people were as lucky as he'd been. *This is lucky?* He wondered. Then *I'd sure hate to see what being unlucky is.*

The sounds coming from the front of the house were growing louder, and his sense of urgency snapped him back to the task at hand. He looked down at the handle and noticed the keyhole in the center, and then it hit him! His grandpa had always kept that door locked, and he hid the key under an old clay jar sitting on the shelf. His Grams had only died less than a year ago, and Luke moved into the house about 3 months after that. Even when spending so much time here as a boy, his grandpa had only taken Luke down into the basement a couple of times to show him some new thing he'd installed or added. Except that one summer when he helped his gramps move a bunch of pipe down there. It was one of those things that his Gramps said was off limits unless he was with him, and it wasn't a place to play. Luke palmed his forehead and ran the few steps back to the shelf, lifted the jar, and snatched up the key. He felt like an idiot for not remembering. But then again, it was a big house, and there were still several rooms Luke hadn't even been through yet since he'd moved in. And he was pretty well panicked when he decided to go to the basement in the first place, so he wouldn't be too hard on himself.

He could hear thumping and scraping sounds, and they were very close. Luke had to get that door open, and pronto! He bounded back to the basement door, and with shaky hands, fumbled with the key for several precious seconds, until at last, the key slid into the keyhole and he pushed down on the handle. It moved downward through its full range, and the door opened with a spooky creaking sound. How long had it been since it was last opened? Gramps had died 9 years ago, and he didn't remember Grams ever going down there, or ever even talking about it.

The smell that wafted out through the door opening was musty and old, but it wasn't at all unpleasant. It was kind of comforting and nostalgic. Not wasting any time, Luke shined his gun's light down the steps and ushered Archie through, but as Luke went through, he was so focused on looking down the stairs that he failed to look up and notice the large spiderweb stretched across the top portion of the doorframe. The spiderweb wrapped almost perfectly around his face as he walked through, and Luke nearly lost it! He never liked spiders to begin with, and the unexpected web across his face made him dance and swat at the sticky, stringy mask wildly. As he grunted and squeaked, Luke lost his footing from the sudden crazy spider dance and went tumbling down the wooden steps. The basement door was *still* open. It all happened so fast, and as Luke lay at the bottom landing, he felt a terrible pain in his left ankle and a stinging sensation in his right elbow and forearm. His pistol rested a couple feet from him with the light shining on the back wall of the basement. Luke looked up the steps that he had just fallen down but couldn't see a thing as there was nothing but blackness up there. He began to panic as he thought of being attacked down here in the basement, trapped, with a hurt ankle, and no way to defend himself. Archie came to his side and licked Luke's face several times in a show of affection and understanding. "Archie, we have to get that door closed," Luke grunted.

Luke tried to stand up, using his good right foot to apply most of his weight as he did, and though he could get to his feet, when he tried to put weight on his left foot, the pain caused him to flinch and pick it up again. "Nope, not happening!" He hopped over to his gun and on one leg, reached down and grabbed it. Archie looked at Luke with a funny cocked expression as he tried to figure out why Luke was hopping on one foot. "I'll be okay, boy, but we gotta get that door closed." Archie danced in circles around Luke, thinking that this was a game, but then, after two more circles, he halted and faced the stairway and growled. His disposition changed with something he had sensed or heard. "Oh crap, let's get up there quick boy!" Luke said, and he hopped to the steps and grabbed the railing with his right hand. His right arm and elbow were hurting, but it was just a gash on his forearm and a skinned elbow. The gash was bleeding, but seemed to slow some. *I'll live,* he thought.

Luke hopped up one step, keeping his left foot off the ground. It was difficult because he was also holding his FNX in his left hand, so they could see up the stairs. The light shined ahead and reflected off the open grey metal door. The doorway was still vacant, thank God. Archie was directly in front of Luke, prowling up the steps as he growled and bristled. "Careful, boy." Luke still couldn't believe the transformation in his playful and loving Shepherd, but Archie's generations of buried instincts were strong, and they were on full display tonight. One more step, then one more. Only eight more steps to go. The light on the FNX was dimming. It wasn't by much, but it was noticeable, and Luke feared that almost as much as he feared the approaching zombies. *Zombies? Really? That's not possible, that's not real.*

Archie barked loudly while curling his lips to reveal his long, sharp teeth, as he paused just four steps from the top. Luke was still three steps behind Archie. The smell hit Luke before the sight of the thing did. Bending around the doorway, a beast of a man presented himself in all his disgusting and putrid glory, and filled the opening at the top of the stairs. The man was enormous and had long stringy hair. He was missing one boot, and was wearing a gray work shirt with his name patch on the front pocket. "Gus?" Luke rasped. This *was* Gus, the mechanic who changed the oil and tires on Luke's truck. Luke would have recognized him anywhere because he looked like the leader of a biker gang, but in reality, he was the nicest guy Luke had ever met. He always had a kind word to say, and he was always smiling. He was truly a gentle giant.

Gus had a gaping hole in the side of his neck, like a giant grape-fruit sized bite had been taken out of it! If this wasn't a zombie, Luke didn't know what would be, because anyone alive would be... well, would be *dead* in this condition. No way Gus could be alive, not in the shape he was in. So is he dead? Luke wondered. Is Gus walking around, *dead?*

Luke shined the light on Gus's face, and he saw the same black eyes looking back at him. Gurgling and hissing emitted from Gus, and then with a quirky cock of his grotesque head, he paused for a moment. Luke could swear that Gus was pondering something. *None of this makes any sense!* Luke thought. Gus's black eyes drifted down the length of Luke and stopped mid-way down for a moment. Then, an awful wailing sound came from deep within Gus, loud and guttural, his eerie gaze frozen on Luke's arm. *The blood!*

Archie charged Gus, driving the giant man backwards, in the unexpected weight of the large Shepherd's momentum. Luke could see Gus stumble a few times backwards before he lost sight of them both. He heard Archie snapping and viciously attacking Gus, though, and Luke tried to hurry to the top of the stairs to better see what was happening, but his right leg was feeling very fatigued from the exertion of hopping up the steps.

Luke heard a loud and painful yelp that he knew came from Archie. "I'm coming boy, hang in there!" Luke yelled. But there was no more snarling or barking, only gurgling sounds, and Luke feared the worst.

Leg burning, Luke hopped up the last two steps, and what he witnessed made him cry out in agony.

Chapter 8

Gus

* * *

G us was working late again. It was the 4th night this week, and he knew his Maggie would be mad at him, because he had missed dinner again, but he had no choice. Mr. Jacobson said he needed his Jeep back by the end of the week for a hunting trip, and this tranny rebuild was good money. Gus had to wait two extra days for the parts to arrive, and that meant he had to work overtime to get it done once they did.

Maggie was a great gal, and Gus loved her dearly. He worked hard because he wanted to make her happy, and give her and little Gus Jr. a good life. His small garage and filling station provided the only income they had, and he just didn't earn enough to hire any help, not yet anyway. Nope, Gus had run this garage all by himself ever since he took it over 11 years ago. He was a good mechanic. No, Gus was a great mechanic, and he'd always wanted to have his own place. And Gus was a savvy guy, for being a country boy, and only having earned his GED.

As a young man of 18, he worked hard to put himself through a local auto mechanic trade school. He was good with his hands, and he could fix just about anything. So working on cars came easy for Gus. When he finished trade school, Gus got a lucky break and was offered a job working as a mechanic for a car dealership. He loved his job, but after spending five years there, more than anything, Gus wanted his own garage. He wanted to be his own man, and when the opportunity came to buy the small filling station on the west side, with only a small down payment, Gus quit his comfortable job at the dealership, and did it. It was hard work, and he made very little money for the first several years. Just about everything he made, Gus had to put back into the garage to make repairs for old, broken down equipment and tools. The lift was the biggest expense... That one set Gus back close to $30,000, and poor Gus needed that lift to work on cars. It took Gus five years to pay off that lift, and he barely scraped by until he did. Everyone loved Gus. He was friendly, honest, and always had a smile on his face. But most of all, he was a darn good mechanic, and it didn't take long for word to get around. His customers always came back, and they told all their friends about Gus.

Gus was a giant of a man, standing 6'6", and weighing nearly 300 pounds. He loved old rock & roll, concert t-shirts, hamburgers, and the Lord. His mama was a strong Christian woman, and she brought Gus to Church every Sunday as a boy, come rain or shine, ever since he could remember. And Gus truly believed that God had his eye on him and was watching over him. He tried to always do good, and would never hurt a soul, though you'd never know it by looking at him. Gus had the look of a wrestler, or the leader of a biker gang. The only thing missing were the tattoos.

One day, a pretty young thing rolled up onto his drive with a flat tire. Gus had been changing out some spark plugs on a Chevy pickup truck when the bell dinged. He walked out onto the drive, wiping his greasy hands on a shop rag when he saw the old beat up Buick with the flat. He shook his head and walked around to the driver's side, and was immediately smitten. There sat the prettiest gal Gus had ever laid eyes on. She smiled shyly at Gus, and Gus's heart melted. He stuttered a bit and said, "Wa... well hello there, miss, looks like you got a tire there that needs fixin'". Gus gave his genuine warm smile right back at her, and she beamed at him.

The conversation from there was slow, awkward, and maybe even a little painful, to anyone else who may have been listening. Those two never knew it though, because they were both enamored with one another. Well, Gus fixed the young lady's flat tire. Margaret was her name, didn't charge her for it, asked her out to dinner, and that was that. They married three months later and bought a small 2-bedroom house that needed more work than the garage Gus had bought 5 years earlier. Margaret, Maggie, as she liked to be called, was a tiny thing, and pretty as a picture, and standing together they looked like a giant and a pixie next to one another. But they loved each other more than any two people in the entire world ever did, and Gus would do anything for Maggie.

Gus loved thinking about that day. It was his favorite memory, and it always made him happy when he did. "Well Gus," he said to himself, "time to get home to that pretty wife of yours". It was now closer to midnight than supper time, and Gus knew he'd get an earful when he got home. He genuinely hated leaving his darling Maggie and their young boy, Gus Jr., home all alone at night, but they needed the money. They had a dream to pay off their little house and then buy a bigger shop, so Gus could then hire some help and really build a successful business. Gus and Maggie only had nine more payments to go, because they had been tripling and even quadrupling their mortgage payment for the past five years. They were so close now they could see their dream coming true. They had to sacrifice a lot over those five years; no going out to dinner, no new car for the family, Gus carrying his lunch to work in a lunch pail like folks did in the olden days, and many other things too. One thing they didn't cut corners on, though, was little Gus Jr. He was their little ray of sunshine. He was four years old now, and Gus Jr. was the most loved little boy there ever was. They spoiled him, that's true, but he was such a loving and sweet little boy, and they doted on him like a little prince. They were a happy little family.

Gus lowered the Jeep on the lift, washed his hands, and packed up his lunch pail and grabbed his keys. He'd test drive the Jeep first thing in the morning and then give Mr. Jacobson a call and let him know it was ready. Gus knew it would drive just fine. He was a great mechanic and never had to do a job twice.

Gus heard sirens off in the distance, and he thought he'd remembered hearing them a few times over the past couple of hours. It was a fleeting thought as he shut off the lights and locked the doors. It was stormy outside and Gus loved the rain, but he hoped his little Gus Jr. wasn't afraid. He should be fast asleep by now, but Gus would be sure to peek in on him when he got home, and quietly give him a goodnight kiss. Gus didn't have an umbrella. He always thought those things were for sissies, but he was sort of wishing he had one now because by the time he made it the few yards to his parked Dodge, he was soaked to the skin. He quickly opened the door, got in, and closed it as fast as he could. Gus set his lunch pail on the bench seat next to him, buckled up, and started the old truck.

He loved his truck. It was like an old friend to him. He'd had it since before he put himself through mechanic's school, and he'd always taken great care of it. It was old even then, but it ran better today than it did back when he was in school. Of course, being a great mechanic and all, he had just about rebuilt the thing twice over since then. It started right up with just the slightest turn of the key. He turned on the lights and windshield wipers and then put on the radio. His favorite rock station, KLKK, was tuned in, but instead of music, the DJ was talking about a plane crash in Mason City. Gus turned it up and put the old truck in reverse to back out of the small space he parked in, in the back. He had a hard time seeing through the back glass with the heavy rain, so he took it slow. He knew he wouldn't hit anything unless something ran or drove behind him and he didn't see it. Gus had backed out of his spot thousands of times over the years, and could do it with his eyes closed. Once he was clear, he put the old column shifter in first gear and started out home.

The rain was coming down harder than he'd ever remembered it here. He had to drive well under the speed limit because he couldn't see worth a darn. He turned up the radio in the old truck as loud as it would go, so he could make out some of what the DJ was saying. The rain was coming down so hard that it sounded like someone was standing over the truck's roof pouring a never-ending bucket of marbles on top of him.

"A plane crash in Mason City? Dang, I can't believe that," Gus said to himself. It was just on the other side of 18 from where they lived, and even closer to his little garage. It was a couple of miles. Even so, it wasn't that far. Yea, them rich folks lived over near there on Country Club Drive. *I sure hope all them folks are okay over there*, Gus thought.

Gus started thinking about Gus Jr., and how he couldn't wait to see him and give him a kiss goodnight. The windshield was fogging up inside, so Gus reached over the steering wheel and tried to wipe it a bit with the back of his hand, but that only helped a little before it fogged up again. He went through this ritual a few more times, but even with his big ole paws, he was still just moving the moisture around and not really wiping it off. After he'd had enough of that, he reached down under his seat for a rag that he thought was down there, but he couldn't feel it. Gus tried again, and stretched even more this time, but as he did, he had to take his eyes off the road for just a moment because he had to turn his head sideways so that he could twist his shoulders enough to get all the way under there. "There you are you danged old rag," Gus muttered in victory, but just as he pinched it between his two fingers and began pulling it out, he felt a hard bump from the front of the truck, then a lurch sideways, and Gus hit the brakes hard. "Dear Lord, what *was* that?" Gus squeaked out in surprise. The truck skidded and bumped hard over something, and Gus hit his head on the ceiling as he rolled over it.

And then Gus did something that he never did. He cursed. "Dammit!" he blurted out.

The old pickup finally came to a stop and Gus sat there for a moment in a bit of a daze. Not because he was hurt, it'd take a lot more than that to hurt Gus's hard ole head, but from the fact that he'd hit something. Gus had never had an accident in his entire life, and he didn't like it at all. It rattled him, and so he just sat there for a minute, listening to the windshield wipers going back and forth, back and forth, in their hypnotic mechanical rhythm. Gus finally got his breathing and heartbeat back to a normal pace and then looked around. First out the front, which was still fogged up, then from side to side, and then through the back glass. Gus couldn't see a dog-gone thing!

A banging sound on the side of the truck, near the back, caught Gus by surprise, and he jumped. Not hard enough to hit his head again, but he sure did a little jig in his seat. "Crap! What the heck is goin' on?" Gus said out loud, drawling out the word "on". The banging continued. It was erratic, but there was no doubt that something or someone was banging on the side of Gus's truck. Gus then feared the worse, "Oh Lord, please, please don't let it be that I hit someone. Please Lord, oh please, no," Gus pleaded.

He knew he'd have to get out in the rain to see what it was, and try to help if he could, and Gus didn't care about that, but he just couldn't bear the thought of seeing someone all broken and bloody because he'd run over them. But his mama didn't raise no coward, and Gus knew what he had to do.

He took one more deep breath to steel himself, and then he opened the door.

The rain was coming down in sheets, and in just a second or two, Gus was soaked to the bone again. He didn't notice, because he was focused on the hand reaching up from the ground to bang on the side of his truck. There was no mistaking that it was a person's hand, and the realization hit Gus with the force of a locomotive, that he'd really run over someone, and now they needed his help. Gus was a strong man, inside and out, so he whispered a little prayer, and moved closer. As things came more and more into focus, Gus looked on in horror at what he'd done. Even through the driving rain, he could see that the lady, yes, it was a woman that he'd run over, was battered and broken in ways that Gus didn't even think possible. Her face was half gone, just as if it were scraped off on the concrete, and her hips and legs were at a 90-degree angle from her torso. She was dragging herself along with one hand and banging on the side of the truck with the other. Gus couldn't understand how the woman was even alive, let alone conscious or moving. He was within arm's reach of the poor broken woman when he saw her eyes for the first time. They were black eyes, completely black. There was no white in her eyes at all, and she wasn't crying, or even screaming, as she looked at Gus. The woman seemed to be trying to say something, because her mouth was moving and her lips were curled up to expose her teeth. Gus thought she was trying to speak, so he knelt down on one knee, close enough to touch her hand. But as he reached for her to comfort her, she grabbed his wrist with such unexpected force, that it pulled Gus off balance, and he teetered forward, falling toward her, and went face down into the puddle that she was laying in on the pavement. He floundered for a moment before he could get his face up out of the water, but his chest was still flat on the ground, so as he looked up, he had to stretch his neck upward. He sort of looked like he was body surfing on his belly, with his hands out in front of him and his neck stretched out in an attempt to keep his head above the water. His right arm was still being pulled hard by the woman just inches from his face now. Gus could see her mouth more clearly now, and he knew she wasn't trying to speak at all, but rather her teeth were moving in a rhythmic biting motion. He briefly wondered if it was some sort of trauma or involuntary nerve reaction caused by being hit by the truck. But then, in a stark moment of realization, time nearly froze, and though it couldn't have been more than a second, Gus could see her teeth descending upon him, in cruel and horrifying slow-motion. And it was in that moment that Gus knew, he just knew - that he was going to die.

Her mouth opened wider than should have been possible, in an almost disjointed and grotesque display. Then, she pulled on Gus's arm with terrifying strength to bring her closer to Gus, and Gus closer to her. He was almost hypnotized while looking into her soulless black eyes, and he had no leverage in his current position to break away. The woman's grip was far more powerful than even his own strength, in his prone and awkward state, and Gus began to weep as he thought of Gus Jr., and his sweet, sweet, Maggie. The woman's mouth almost seemed to wrap around the side of Gus's neck as he felt her teeth effortlessly rip through his skin and sink in deep. He heard her moan in delight and sated bliss, loudly against his flesh, and the pain was like nothing Gus had ever felt before. It was ripping, pulling, and tearing his flesh, and he could feel his insides bubbling out into this woman's, this thing's mouth, and dripping down his collarbone and shoulder. But he *could not* scream! Even though his mouth was open and his guts were churning, no sound came from Gus. But tears did, as he thought of his sweet Maggie and little Gus Jr.

Then merciful numbness and a kind of tranquility settled over Gus, and he was so very thankful for that. He could feel his heartbeat slowing, and he closed his eyes against the rain, and his own tears. Then, all sound left him and he was suddenly in a dark and quiet place, with no feeling, no sound, no anything, and his heartbeat stopped. He was somehow aware of that, and a fog slowly veiled his thoughts. His understanding, and all feeling, left old Gus. But there was something new now. It was primal; it was all-consuming, and it was absolute. Gus was hungry!

Chapter 9

Heartbreak

* * *

"**A**rchie! Gus, no!" Luke bellowed out in a horse growl. Luke looked on in heartbreaking horror at the combined mass of Gus and Archie, as Gus was squeezing the breath and life from his beloved companion in a vise-like bear hug as Archie dangled there in his iron embrace. Luke could see Archie's eyes. They were open and looking right at Luke with an anguished and pleading sadness. That look was simply more than Luke could bear, and a flood of tears spilled from Luke's eyes. But then, a beast awakened within *him*. Adrenaline coursed through him, and Luke lost all awareness of his own pain-racked body. He put his foot down and charged at Gus with every bit of speed and strength his battered body could muster, and it was formidable. Luke was an athletic man, and charged with anger, fear, and pure hatred for this man who was taking his Archie from him. He plowed into Gus's shoulder with the force of a charging bull. The impact with the cold blobby mass of Gus was like hitting a giant side of beef in a butcher's meat locker, but just the same, Gus toppled sideways to the ground, with Archie still in his embrace. The impact jarred Archie loose from Gus, and Archie was able to weakly scramble away from Gus's outstretched hands. Gus floundered ridiculously on the floor and moaned and hissed like a raging man who had gone completely mad.

They had little time, because they could not hope to keep Gus down. He was too big, too strong, and Luke and Archie were both in bad shape. Luke couldn't possibly get to his gun, which held the light, and to Archie, so there was only one thing to do, and that was to somehow get himself and Archie through that basement door, and close it before Gus could get to them. With adrenaline still pumping, Luke hobbled as fast as he could to his weakened companion and scooped him up into his arms as gingerly as he could. As he held his Shepherd in his arms, Luke could barely see where he was going, with just the faintest of light from the gun illuminating the large room, and with Archie in his arms blocking his view. Archie whimpered almost inaudibly, and then they both heard and felt the pounding on the floor behind them. The grunts and moans coming from the behemoth, Gus, were inhuman and replete with agony and need. Luke knew Gus wanted them, well wanted him anyway, and somehow he knew Gus wanted to end him, to *eat* him.

Gus was on his feet now, and only 20 feet from Luke and Archie, and he was lumbering towards them in that now familiar mechanical shuffle. He was hissing and gurgling now and the smell of the stinking beast filled the room and was making Luke's eyes water. Luke was stumbling toward the basement opening with the full dead weight of Archie in his arms, making it hard to balance without falling forward. Archie was a heavy boy. Luke could just make out the silhouette of the half-opened door.

He didn't think they were going to make it. It was like in one of those awful dreams, where you try to run from something, but it was as if your feet weren't your own and simply wouldn't obey. You just couldn't move fast enough, like trudging through mud that's up to your knees. Luke was barely moving, it seemed, and he could feel the tremors on the floor, in a rhythm with the disgusting sounds, and they were so very close now. Luke didn't dare try to look behind them, though, to spend the precious energy and time to turn and see where Gus was, but he fully expected the beast to slam into him from behind at any moment and knock them both to the ground. He knew that would be the last thing he would feel before Gus bit into him and began pulling his flesh from his body while he watched in helpless horror.

"No!" Luke yelled at the thought and lunged forward with another surge he didn't know he had in him. That was enough, though, to just get them to the door. But in that same moment, he felt the tips of Gus's giant fingertips graze his shoulder from behind, like a ghoulish hand reaching from a grave. And just as Luke knew he would, he fell forward from the involuntary jerk at the feel of the grotesque Gus upon him, and he and Archie hit the ground hard. Their forward momentum caused Archie to slide to the edge of the stairwell, and then Luke heard him thump and roll down the stairs. There was a slight yelp as the tumbling sound grew faint, and then stopped entirely.

Luke wasn't so lucky. His right shoulder hit the narrow butt end of the door that was swung open just so, to face him, like an awaiting axe blade. The pain was agonizing, and Luke's scream came involuntarily along with the pain. Worse, Gus was now upon him, and Luke could scarcely form a coherent thought through the pain that overwhelmed him. He couldn't see Gus. All he could see was a mass of blackness where he thought Gus should be. Luke seethed through clenched teeth, and with eyes watering from both the smell of Gus and his own pain, he kicked out hard with his right foot and connected with an invisible wall that he knew must be there.

The crunch was loud and sickening, and his foot didn't stop at the contact, but rather kept on going straight through. And then an enormous quake shook the floor as the stinking mass hit the hardwood with the force of a grand piano. Luke had somehow connected full on with one of Gus's legs, and from the feel of it, it snapped right in two. There was silence for a few moments, followed by a dragging sound on the floor. Luke couldn't see, but his mind's eye painted the only picture he needed to get him moving. Luke stretched for the door handle, or maybe the large L-shaped metal latch that was welded to the inside of the door. Anything, hoping to grab onto something so he could pull himself through.

His grandpa had installed a 4-inch hinged metal bar that would swing down from the inside and drop down tightly into the metal latch and across the doorjamb. It would take a charging rhinoceros to break down that door from the outside when that bar was in place. But the moment Luke's fingers gained purchase on the handle, an iron hand wrapped around his left ankle and pulled him in the opposite direction. The agony of Luke's already swollen ankle was almost more than he could bear. He was so broken and battered in so many places, and just wanted to get to safety so that he could try to figure out what was happening, and to take care of Archie. But Gus had his own plans.

Luke cocked his right foot again, and kicked out with all the force he could gather, but he didn't connect with anything at all this time, and realized that Gus must be stretched out as well. Luke couldn't pull his left leg either, because the pain was excruciating. He didn't know what to do. If he kicked at the hand holding him, he'd most likely kick his own ankle and the pain was already a 10 out of 10 on the pain scale. But then, Gus began pulling even harder, and Luke yelled in utter agony at the increased pain. Okay, so maybe it was a 9 out of 10 before, but now, it was definitely 10. It truly felt as if Gus was going to pull his foot right off, just snap it off at the ankle.

Luke heard a soft padding on the stairs, and then a warm lick on his face. His loyal Archie was somehow there, again, to help his master.

Luke was dizzy with pain and was barely holding on. Archie bolted away and Luke heard a vicious snarling sound as his ankle was being yanked from side to side by Gus's iron grip. Archie must have seized Gus's arm, because though the pulling pressure was now gone, a wild side-to-side motion ensued. In an instant, the iron grip released

Luke's ankle, and Luke moaned in relief. He said a silent prayer and then called Archie to him with the strongest voice he could command. It wasn't much.

"Archie, come, boy!"

Luke pulled himself up the best he could as he strained to hold on to the door handle. He felt Archie's head against his thigh and grabbed the scruff of his neck, and panted out, "Thanks boy, let's get inside now!" He pushed Archie through the door, and Luke followed, as he slammed it shut behind them, and dropped the metal bar down with a loud metallic clang.

Total darkness engulfed them.

Chapter 10

The Basement

* * *

Luke collapsed, nearly lifeless, on the tiny landing just inside the door. He could feel Archie's head on his chest. They were both panting, utterly spent. Luke could barely think, for the pain and weariness that he felt, and his legs were dangling awkwardly over the first step, but he didn't care. It was dark too, but he didn't care about that either. This moment of peace and safety, away from those, those *things*, was all he needed, all he wanted. He intended to savor it for as long as he could. Besides, he had no strength to do anything else, anyway. So he closed his eyes and lay his hand atop of Archie's big head. Archie seemed perfectly content to lie right there, too.

"I love you, boy," Luke rasped softly, and then he fell asleep.

Bang! Scratch! Bang! The sounds were violent, and with no sort of pattern. They were just persistent and erratic. And they were on the door right next to his head. It was so dark... Luke was fuzzy at first, and he didn't remember where he was. His chest was hot and a little sore from where Archie still lay on him. He blinked a few times, but that didn't help him see at all, so he attempted to push himself up into a sitting position, when the pain in his right shoulder stopped him. Then it all came rushing back to him. In an instant, Luke knew exactly where they were and what they had been through. He wanted to close his eyes again and just forget for a little while longer, when Archie stirred a bit and lifted his head. Luke tried to sit again, this time pushing up using his left hand. He managed it this time, and he put his back against the door as he did so. The banging continued from the other side of the door, but Luke didn't pay any attention to it. He knew they were safe. Gramps had built a war-time bunker down here, and nothing was coming through that door, not unless Luke opened it first.

"Big Bear, it's dark, boy. You okay?" Luke whispered.

Bark!

Luke gently scratched Archie behind his ears.

"What do you think about trying to get down these stairs and finding something to drink? Want some water, boy?"

Bark! Bark!

Archie knew the familiar word, and he needed some as much as Luke did. They were both on the verge of dehydration. "Well, I need to see if I can stand up first. Watch out, I'm gonna be a bit wobbly, and I really don't want to step on you."

He knew that Archie probably didn't have any idea what the heck he was saying, but it made Luke feel better just to talk to Archie, and he knew that somehow, it made Archie feel better, too. Archie knew some words pretty well, but Luke was certain that it must have sounded something like, *blah blah blah* "water", blah blah blah blah "outside", blah blah blah "cookie". But neither one cared. They loved each other, and that was all that mattered. It was something Luke had only ever read about, or maybe he'd seen it in a movie, but he never thought he'd feel such a thing. Not until Archie came along. Now he understood what it all meant. Archie was more than a dog. He was Luke's best friend, and he loved him more than he thought it was possible to love a dog. That's because to Luke,

Archie wasn't just a dog, he was family, his loyal and loving companion.

The banging on the door grew more agitated at the sound of Archie's bark and Luke's voice.

"Hey boy, I'm going to stand up now and see how that feels. Watch out, okay?"

Luke reached above his head and grabbed onto the cold steel bar that securely held the door. Luke thought to himself as he wrapped his fingers around it. *This is the only thing keeping us alive...* He patted it a couple of times thoughtfully. He then took a deep breath and steeled himself for a whole lot of pain that he knew was coming, and then he hoisted himself up. Surprised that it wasn't nearly as bad as he expected it to be, Luke put a little weight on his left foot to test it out, but quickly picked it up again. "Nope!" he grunted.

"Hey Big Bear, down the stairs boy, go on now. Move, so I don't trip over you." He gave Archie a little nudge on his backside. Archie seemed to understand, and soon after, Luke heard his paws on the stairs as he descended them. Luke was thoughtful for a moment, as he listened to Archie pad down the stairs. He wondered at how Archie didn't seem to mind the darkness at all. He guessed that his superior sense of hearing and smell had a lot to do with it. Luke could hide something from Archie after they played with it for a few minutes, and no matter where he hid it, once he gave the search command, Archie would put his nose to the ground and find it every time, without fail. He had such an intense focus on finding that object, too. If it was out of reach, or behind something that Archie couldn't move, he would sit there and bark until Luke came to assist. Luke loved that game with Archie. He taught him that when he was a puppy, and that's when Luke realized how intelligent Archie truly was. Tonight, Archie proved that over and over again.

Luke smiled at the thought. He leaned forward to feel for the railing, grabbed it, and began the slow and arduous descent down the steps. As he did, he crooned a cheerful song between panting breaths, to let Archie hear he was okay and in good spirits. Luke liked to sing, and he knew he wasn't very good at it, but he liked it all the same. And Archie always knew Luke was in a good mood when he did. It was important to Luke right now to let Archie know that all was okay, that they would be *okay*.

We will be okay, won't we, Lord? Luke said a silent prayer.

As Luke made it to the last step, he plopped down to rest his burning right leg. "I'm good, Archie, just need to rest boy," he panted out to his companion. Archie was right there, as Luke reached his hand out to touch his soft fur.

"We need to find some light, and then find something to drink."

Luke hadn't been down in Grandpas's basement in a very long time, but he remembered a few things that his gramps showed to him. Grandpa had put a water filtration system down there that ran through some big carbon filters and into a sink. *That*, he remembered, was tied into the old house's plumbing. One summer, as a boy, he had helped his grandpa carry loads and loads of copper pipe and other supplies down here, when he built that filtration system, and a small bathroom. Gramps also had two or three giant shiny gravity fed water tanks with filters inside of them, and dozens of 5-gallon jugs of water stacked against the wall next to them.

His grandpa used to always say, "One is none and two is one."

Luke never forgot that, not really because he thought it meant something important back then, but because it sounded kinda funny when Gramps said it. "One is none and two is one," Luke said aloud.

Luke knew they had plenty of water down there, even if the town's water stopped working, and he was thankful for that. But he had to find a light first, and that was the other thing Luke remembered. Gramps had always kept a shelf at the bottom of the stairs, lined with candles, flashlights, matches, and a bunch of other junk. He told Luke that the important things you might need right away should be close to the entrance, so that when you needed them, you wouldn't have to go *hunting* for them. Luke also remembered that his grandpa had stored enough food down there to feed a small army.

Those were the things that stuck in Luke's mind the most. And right now, he was thankful for that, and for his grandpa!

Grabbing the handrail with his left hand, Luke pulled hard to get back onto his feet. Well, foot anyway. It was so dark down here, he couldn't even see his hand in front of his face. He didn't think he could stand this kind of darkness much longer before he started seeing things, so finding a source of light was his priority. Luke placed his palm flat on the cold cinderblock wall to his left and leaned against it while standing on his right foot. He inched his way along, because he knew that the shelf was close by, and he didn't want to ram his one good hand or arm into it. Luke slowly slid his hand forward along the wall, just enough so that he didn't lose his balance, then he took a small hop on his right foot to come up next to that point on the wall. He repeated this three times, until on the fourth try, as his hand slid gently forward, he touched the large set of shelves. Luke practically yelled in elated victory, "I found it, boy!" Archie came up next to him and brushed his leg with his side. "Now, to find us a light."

Luke hobbled his way around to the front of the set of shelves and began gingerly sliding his hand along the one at chest level. His hand hit something hard, but it wasn't a light. It didn't take him long to figure out it was a rifle of some sort. He kept searching with his hand as far as he could reach. There wasn't anything on that shelf that felt like a light or candle. But he felt some small heavy boxes, which he decided were shells of some sort, and a long-bladed knife, or a machete that was inside a sheath.

Luke didn't want to hop anymore until he absolutely had to, so he reached up one shelf higher from where he stood. He found a tall pillar candle almost immediately. He then felt next to it and found a lighter. "Yes!" He yelled, and Archie barked in surprise.

Luke grabbed the candle and set it on the lower shelf in front of him, the one that held the rifle. He then reached up for the lighter. It was one of those long lighters with a trigger. He pulled on it with his index finger, but the darn thing wouldn't budge. He squeezed it again and nothing happened, not even a click. "No, no, no," Luke sighed in disappointment, thinking that it was so old that it must have frozen up. Then he felt foolish for not remembering that those things always had a child safety on them somewhere. He quickly found the button on the top to push forward with his thumb, and he lit the lighter with one small click.

The illumination from that single flame was almost like finding a lifeboat in a stormy ocean. The feeling of relief that washed over Luke was like a tidal wave. His lip quivered a bit with all the unexpected emotion that he suddenly felt. But then, he felt a little silly again, so he looked down at Archie and smiled at him. "It's good to see you again, boy!" he said, as he lit the candle.

Though Luke was so thrilled to have Archie by his side, and to finally reach safety, he knew they needed water, and fast. He took a cursory glance at the shelf in front of him and said a silent thank you to his grandpa. On the middle shelf there sat a 12-Gauge pump shotgun and several boxes of oo buckshot. There was also a machete, a Beretta 92FS handgun, and several boxes of hollow-point ammo for it, too. Luke looked up to the next shelf where he found the candle and discovered a couple of flashlights sitting about a foot further along the shelf. He shook his head and smiled. He grabbed one flashlight, flicked it on, and then turned away from the shelf to look around the large room. Right away, he spotted the water bottles and chrome water tanks along the left wall, about 15 feet from where he stood, and began hopping over to them. Archie was panting, and Luke knew his pup was thirsty. "Come on, boy, let's go get you some water." As they made their way over, Luke stopped about halfway for a moment, and again wondered how he was going to give Archie water from the supply he spotted. He made a turn to head towards the small bathroom along the back wall instead. It was further, but he knew there was a sink in there, and hopefully something to put water in for Archie to drink out of. Winded and aching, he was losing his balance after a few more hops, so he had to stop and lean on the table that sat near the center of the room for a few moments. Archie looked up at him.

Bark! Bark!

"I'm okay boy, I'm just aching all over and needed a rest," Luke huffed out between breaths. He noticed a couple of doors, and several more shelving units along the wall just past the bathroom entrance, that he'd never seen before. Of course, it had been many years since he had been down here, but he was sure he'd remember those. "Looks like Gramps stayed busy down here after I went to college," he said aloud, and then ruffled Archie's head. "Let's get to that water, boy." After only five more hops, Luke made it to the bathroom door, and he shined the light inside. The door was open, so he didn't have to turn the doorknob while holding the light in the same hand. As he walked in, he noticed that the room was larger than he remembered. He didn't take the time to look around. For now, he made his way directly to the sink. There was a shelf, just to the left of the mirror that was over the sink, and resting on the shelf were four Tupperware style containers with lids, each holding various bathroom supplies. Luke set the flashlight down on the countertop, with the beam facing the wall, and grabbed the nearest one, dumping the contents out onto the counter. There were several tubes of toothpaste in this one. Luke placed the bowl in the sink and turned on the cold water faucet. He was thankful that the water came on right away, but the water that came out was murky brown, and it smelled. He knew Gramps ran the water down here through a large filter system so he couldn't understand why the water looked and smelled like stagnant creek water. But before he could think of what to do next, the water flowed cold and clear. Luke breathed a sigh of relief and emptied the bowl and rinsed it with the clean water. Then he filled it and did his best to lean over and place it on the floor without spilling it. That part didn't go so well, but at least half of it remained in the large bowl, and Archie didn't seem to mind at all that the other half was in a puddle by his feet. Archie's big tongue quickly lapped up the water, and then he began licking the floor. Luke picked up the bowl as quickly as his aching body would allow him, filled it again, and set it back down in front of Archie, this time with a little more grace than the first time. Archie again emptied the bowl, and looked up at Luke. "Okay, Big Bear, let's take it slow now. I'm sure it's not good for you to drink so much, so fast. I'm going to get a drink for myself, and then have a look at these battered bones of mine. Then I'll give you some more. Deal?" Luke said compassionately. Archie began licking the floor again. Luke shook his head, but then decided that the floor was a lot cleaner than those grody people that Archie had been chewing on for the past hour, and just let him do his thing.

Luke bent his head down to the stream of water coming out of the faucet, but with him standing on only one foot, and with one of his arms also out of commission, it was awkward and too painful for him. He grabbed the cup on the sink's counter that was holding several toothbrushes, turned it over so that they fell onto the countertop, and then filled the cup with water. He didn't even bother rinsing it out first, he just filled it up and gulped it down. After three more full cups, he still wanted more, but decided he should probably slow down, too.

Archie had finished cleaning the floor by now and was laying down, looking up at Luke. "That sure hit the spot, huh boy." Archie laid his head down flat on the floor, and gravity made his face and lips droop just so that he looked as if he had more lips and skin than he was supposed to; they just sort of flattened out there on the floor. He looked like a big ole goofy hound dog, and not the handsome German Shepherd that he really was. Luke was glad he was resting and that he seemed to be okay. He'd been watching Archie as they made their way to the bathroom, and he didn't seem to limp or anything. Luke was so glad for that, but there was a long scratch on the inside of one of his ears that he'd clean and look at later. But first, he had to see how bad of shape he was in. If how he felt was any sign, then it had to be pretty bad.

Luke moved the flashlight to point upward. He noticed a couple of candles sitting on the shelf above the bowls and decided it would be better if he lit one of those. Of course, there was a lighter sitting there too, so he lit both of them. He didn't want to waste them, but he really needed to see right now, so he decided it was okay. He'd blow them out as soon as he finished looking himself over. The light was better now, and not so concentrated in a single beam like the flashlight made. As he turned back to the mirror, Luke almost didn't recognize himself. His face was filthy, hair disheveled, and his right shoulder was bleeding through his t-shirt. Aside from the blood being red instead of black, he thought he almost looked like one of those things that he and Archie had been running from all night. Luke had to reposition himself because his right leg was burning from the fatigue of holding all of his weight for so long. He plopped down onto the closed toilet seat cover and moaned in relief. "Oh man, that's better!" Then he pulled his aching left ankle across his right thigh, and pulled off the warm sock, and as he did, he noticed that it too now had and a big hole in the heel. "That's just great!" he huffed in mock irritation. He rubbed his ankle gingerly and felt around to see if anything was sticking out. It was a little puffy, but otherwise, he felt nothing out of the ordinary. He grabbed the flashlight from the counter and shone it on his ankle to give it a closer look. Yep, swollen, and a bit of a bruise was forming above his instep, but otherwise, it didn't look too bad. He was glad it didn't seem to be more than a sprain, but he'd remembered reading that sprains could be pretty bad too, if they were severe enough. Massaging it a little, he tried to rotate it some using his left hand. Though he could tolerate a little motion, he decided not to overdo it for now, so he put his *holey* sock back on.

After a brief rest, he pulled his shirt over his head. That was a monumental task, given he could barely move his right arm without a great deal of pain. Truthfully, he was more worried about his shoulder than his ankle at the moment. It just didn't feel right, and he knew something was wrong in there. Once he got his shirt off, which took a good long minute, he took a deep breath and hoisted himself up, using the countertop for leverage and balance. He again looked into the mirror, and right away he saw the long gash on top of his

71

shoulder, and it was caked with thick, dried blood. He picked up the light and tried to get a better look, but again, nothing seemed to poke out the wrong way anywhere that he could see. But that gash was deep, and he thought it was going to need stitches or it would heal badly. When he tried to move his arm, he could see the gash open up some, causing the severe pain he was feeling.

Luke set the flashlight down and turned the water back on. He picked up as much water as he could in his cupped left hand and began splashing the wound to clean it up some. After several minutes, and a lot of clenching of teeth and grunting, he was able to get most of the old blood off, and the wound looked mostly clean now. But it was bleeding again, not a lot, but enough that he knew he had to find a bandage or something, to at least cover it for now. Using the hand towel next to the sink, he dabbed at his shoulder. He hated getting blood all over it, but he figured Gramps would understand.

He had to take a break, so he sat back down on the toilet again and shone his flashlight around the room. Luke looked in wonder around the large bathroom, and his respect for his grandpa flew up another few notches. It was already pretty high, so that was saying something. That old man had somehow dug out another twenty feet or so, and now the bathroom was three times the size that Luke remembered. Luke couldn't even imagine the engineering that went into that project, but he knew it wasn't as simple as digging a hole. He had to support the weight of the earth above as he moved large amounts of dirt out of here. But where did he put it all? And how did he move it? And how did he do this all by himself? Luke had so many questions, but he might never know the answers. His gramps was strong, but he was in his 70s when Luke went off to College. "Grandpa, you're amazing! I sure do miss you," Luke softly whispered. As he looked around with the flashlight, Luke spotted a big white metal cabinet on one wall in the expanded area that had a large red cross on it. "Thank you, Jesus," Luke said, and he stood up and began hopping over to it. Archie stirred a bit, lifted his head, and turned it enough to see his master moving to the other side of the room. But he decided that all was okay, so he laid his head back down and closed his eyes. Luke made it over in a few short hops, and he leaned against the wall for a moment, resting on the flashlight. There was nothing to put the flashlight on nearby, so he had to set it on top of the large first aid cabinet. There was plenty of light from that, and the candles on the other side of the bathroom. He flipped open the two large metal latches on the side of the cabinet and swung the door open. He quickly found some antibiotic ointment, a package of gauze, and some medical tape, and shoved them all into his sweatpants pocket. Gramps had stocked this cabinet with just about everything you could think of; sutures, glue, eye wash, bandaids, sheers, iodine, alcohol, peroxide, gauze of every size, and some small white tubes labeled WoundSeal. Luke grabbed a couple of those too and put them into his pocket. He also grabbed a bottle of superglue; he remembered reading in a book once where someone had used super-glue to close a wound. Luke also shoved a roll of stretchy ace bandage into his pocket.

Gramps lined the top shelf of the cabinet with rows of amber bottles labeled with various drug names. Luke saw a couple that he recognized and snatched them up. One said Amoxicillin, which he knew was an antibiotic, and another was Tylenol with codeine. He stuck those in his pocket too, and then he grabbed the flashlight and hopped back over to the toilet to sit back down. Luke was exhausted, and really just wanted to sleep, but he had to get this cut of his treated and bandaged up before he could rest.

He pulled the things he'd gathered out of his pockets, and he placed them down on the counter next to him. One bottle of medicine fell to the floor and rolled behind the toilet. Luke sighed. He would have to get that later, but he told himself to take it slow. He was punchy and tired, and he was being a little careless. It would take him twice as long to get this done if he didn't slow down and concentrate. He picked up the package of gauze and opened it and was happy to see that there were several large squares inside. He took one and began softly patting the wound to soak up some of the fresh blood. After a few pats, he set the bloody piece on the counter, then grabbed a clean one and put it down on his lap. Then he picked up one of the small white tubes of WoundSeal and tried to read the label, but the light was too dim to make out the small writing. He opened it with his teeth and gently poured a small amount out onto his pant leg to look at it. It seemed pretty straightforward, and he couldn't think of anything else to do with it, other than to just pour the stuff directly on the gash. He sure hoped that's what he was supposed to do with it. "Well, here goes nothin'," he murmured. It stung a little, but not too much. He waited a few minutes for the bleeding to stop and he rested his weary eyes. It didn't take long at all and it amazed Luke how well the powder had worked. He took a clean piece of gauze and again cleaned the wound the best he could. Then, as he struggled to open the small tube of superglue, he remembered once as a kid how he had glued his fingers together. He certainly didn't want to do that again, so he was as careful as he could be *not* to do that again. Thankfully, the tube had a long pointy tip so that he could easily direct it to a specific place. Once he got the seal off and the pointy tip back on, he carefully squeezed a tiny bead along the gash. It stung badly, and he was afraid it would start bleeding again, so he quickly dropped the tube onto the counter and pinched the two sides of the gash together, careful to squeeze from as far away from the gash as possible, to avoid touching it and gluing his fingertips to his shoulder. After holding it for a minute, he let go, and to his surprise, it held fast. He picked up the tube of antibiotic ointment and squirted out a long thick line of the goopy stuff onto another clean piece of gauze, and he positioned it over the long gash, and pressed it down softly. The ointment held it in place while he rested for a few moments. Maybe it was all in his head, but he could swear that it already felt a lot better. It was tedious, but he managed to tear several strips of tape from the roll, and tape the gauze down to his skin. It was sloppy, but it would do. His neck was hurting from looking at his shoulder for so long, as he worked at bandaging it up.

All patched up and exhausted, Luke stood up and filled his cup with water again and gulped it down. Archie lifted his head and looked at Luke with hopeful eyes. "Okay Big Bear, you can have more water now too".

Luke didn't know how much time had passed since he started looking himself over. Maybe an hour or more? He wasn't sure. But at least it was done. He steadied himself and squatted down and grasped the empty bowl with his right hand, while keeping his arm straight, and then stood up again and grabbed it with his left hand. This seemed to work out pretty well, so he filled it with water and put it back down the same way. "That was easy, boy. Shoulda done it that way the first time," Luke said, as he smiled down at Archie, who made quick work of the water. Luke picked up the one amber bottle that still sat on the counter and read the label. It was the Tylenol with codeine. He was relieved, because he wanted to take a couple to ease some of his aches and pains. He had to lower the bottle to his right hand, hold it there, and twist the lid with his left hand. That hurt some, but he tossed a couple of tablets into his mouth and then drank another cup of water. What Luke needed most now was to lie down, and so decided he didn't have enough energy to find the cots that he knew his gramps must have down here somewhere. He instead hopped over to the shelf lined with towels, grabbed an armful, and hopped back over to Archie and sat down on the toilet again. With a little effort, Luke spread one towel out on the floor. It was a large towel, and he was thankful for that. He dropped two more towels onto the floor next to it. Standing once more, Luke blew out one candle, then lowered himself down onto the towel spread out next to Archie. He positioned one of the folded towels to use as a pillow, and he did his best to spread the other over himself as a blanket. It didn't quite cover him, but it would do.

With Archie nuzzled against Luke's left side, it was easy for Luke to lay his arm across Archie. "Hey boy, this is just like camping, huh?" Luke whispered. Then he thought of the hunting trip they were planning to take together, and how the nights would probably be a lot like this. Archie rolled over onto his back, hoping for a good belly scratch from his master. Luke knew Archie must have been feeling okay if he wanted a belly scratch.

They sure looked a sight, laying there on the bathroom floor in his grandpa's basement, Luke all beat to crap, and Archie, laying next to him on his back.

His final thought was of his Gramps, and how thankful he was for what he had built down here, before he drifted off into a deep sleep.

Chapter 11

Jonah

* * *

P ure fear drove Jonah as fast as his 265 pound frame could move. His lungs burned and his heart pounded harder and faster than he could ever remember. He had to put as much distance between him, and those... those things, and that's all that mattered. Jonah was crashing into open half-built production machines, and throwing carts and ladders carelessly, violently even, as he raced for the end of the long line. This new Jell-O Pudding production facility was the length of 3 football fields, and two of those things were just behind him. He knew that if they caught him, they would pull him down and do... well, do what they did to poor Ted. He could *not* let that happen. No freaking way! He wouldn't hesitate to take a bullet for any of his squad in the war, but he could not comprehend being eaten alive.

Jonah just couldn't push that scene, or Ted's screams out of his head. He had watched that crazed man and woman tear strips of flesh from Ted's convulsing body and begin chewing savagely, as the blood and juices gushed from their mouths. Jonah had seen nothing like that before, not even during his four deployments in the Middle East, and he had seen plenty there! But witnessing the couple, with those lifeless black eyes, biting, ripping, and chewing strands of meat and muscle from Ted, as he kicked and screamed, was more than Jonah could process. Ted's screams were other-worldly and racked with unbelievable pain and horror.

Tears were still streaming down Jonah's face as he rounded the corner and then fell hard as he tried to take the corner too fast. The production facility's exit was in his sights as he heard the groans and gangly footsteps coming up behind him.

This was a large Jell-O and Jell-O Pudding production facility, and this new line was going to be the largest one in the plant. The next largest one would only be half this size, and Jonah ran the length of it, because he had been working on the automation systems in the control room when all hell broke loose. Trapped in that control room, Jonah had no other escape except to break a large plate-glass window and dive through it, after seeing poor Ted being eaten alive. Two more of the crazed people had just entered the large double glass doors into the control room as Jonah threw the heavy stool through the window. The sound caused them to jerk their heads toward Jonah, and the chase was on.

Jonah just couldn't understand what was happening. Why were these freaks acting this way?

Jonah got to his feet as fast as he could, and after what seemed like long minutes, he finally burst through the plant's exit doors. Blood-curdling screams and chaos filled his senses the moment he hit the open air, but Jonah grabbed an orange construction sign post that was placed in a bucket outside the door and rammed the pole through the door handles hoping that would buy him a little more time. Then, a freaking *bus* hit him impossibly hard on his blind side; at least it felt like a bus, and once again, splayed Jonah on the ground as he hit the pavement like a giant sack of wet sand. And before he could even comprehend the moment, something was on top of him. The hard fall rattled him, and his senses weren't fully with him yet, but he knew enough to understand that he had less than a second to stop this thing before its stinking, rotting breath and teeth were directly upon his neck. Jonah used his formidable strength to bring his right knee up with all that he was worth and drove it into the thing's side. The forced expulsion of air that was inside of it accompanied the grossly inhuman grunt that came from the thing, and it spewed toward Jonah's face before the thing flew off him. The stench was like rotting death, which sadly, Jonah had smelled far too often when in Uncle Sam's service. He heaved and almost yarked. But then there was something else, something he couldn't quite put his finger on, but he decided that now was not the time to figure it out. Jonah pushed himself up and tried to take in the scene before him. But before he could register anything, the man-thing was coming at Jonah again, so Jonah turned slightly and leaned back on his left leg while lifting and kicking high and out with his right. He perfectly timed the kick with the man's approach, and Jonah's heal connected with its chin at the peak of momentum. The sickening crunch was unmistakable, and the man's feet came off the ground as he flew backward through the air. Jonah saw the unnatural angle of the man's head and neck before he hit the ground, and knew that he would not be getting back up again. Jonah turned to run, but as he did, three more were upon him. "This is crazy!" Jonah yelled. "What's wrong with you people?" he screamed. There was no response, just dead black eyes fixated on him, and the creepy figures coming at him fast. They moved so unnaturally and Jonah couldn't figure out why, but he understood he had to move, and move now!

Jonah assessed his situation. Behind him were the doors he'd just come out of, and they were giving way fast to the powerful and frantic pounding on the other side. To his left was a solid brick wall, and to his right there were at least a dozen more freak people shuffling toward him. Jonah saw that his only way out of this was straight ahead, so he lowered his shoulder like he did when he played on the O-line in high-school, and catapulted himself at the three... whatever they were. They were now only about 5 meters away and his only plan now was to plow through them and try to make it to his truck, then he'd figure out what to do next. When Jonah made impact, it was like hitting three giant bags of cold meat. It was an odd sensation, and not like he remembered when playing football with pads crunching. All three went down like bowling pins, and Jonah just kept on running. The impact had smeared some of their, whatever it was, all over his shirt. It was black and rancid, and it made him gag as he ran.

Jonah realized he was on the wrong side of the building and would not be able to get to his pickup truck easily. It was at the other end of the new construction and on the other side. "Well, crap!" Jonah blurted out in frustration. He pointed himself in the right direction and broke into a full on run. Jonah was in great shape, he always stayed fit, and for a big guy, he ran like a track star. Running was easy for Jonah. He ran at least 20 miles a week, and more if the weather and his schedule would let him. As good a shape as he was in while in high school, Ranger School, and later, during his deployments, with Jonah's continuous training, he never lost it. This was nothing for him. The fact that whatever the hell these things were, were trying to eat him, just made him run all the faster. Jonah's mind was reeling as he tried to understand what was happening.

As he ran, he tried to put the pieces together to help him make some sense of it all. Then he thought of Luke, and with the force of an M1A1 Abrams tank, it hit Jonah right between the eyes. "Black eyes!" Jonah huffed as he ran. He remembered what Luke had been so freaked out by on that news report. *No freaking way!* Jonah couldn't believe that was related to this mess, but nothing else made sense. Those eyes were the big clue, and he had seen plenty of them tonight. *These people are infected with something!* He thought as he rounded the corner of the extensive building. When Jonah saw what was on the other side, he dropped to the ground as fast as he could, and stared in disbelief.

Chapter 12

Cornered

* * *

Jonah tried to slow his breathing, and he got as small as he could down on the ground. The long run had him winded, and there wasn't much of anything to hide behind except for a few inches of wild grass. It was the only thing that separated him from the enormous expanse of pavement that lay just 15 meters in front of him. He could hear his breaths, and his own heartbeat in his head, and he was afraid the horde of meatheads that he'd almost run right smack into would hear it too.

Oh, crap oh crap oh crap, did they see me? Please please please, no...

He wasn't sure what he'd do if they saw him. Jonah peeked above the grass that he prayed concealed him, but he felt like an elephant trying to hide under a gum wrapper. There was no way they didn't see him, but none seemed to move toward him though. Jonah wasn't sure what his next move should be. He knew that several of these things that he'd left behind were now tracking him. They were still pretty far back the last time he looked over his shoulder, but they didn't seem to give up. He was sure they would be on him within the next few minutes.

Not 10 meters in front of Jonah was a horde of the frenzied people. The parking lot was crawling with dozens of them, walking this way and that, and a few piles of them down on the ground, busy with something, *or someone*. The stench wafting his way was dizzying. He tried to think of what this could all mean and what had happened to them all, but he didn't want to believe what his mind was telling him. It just wasn't possible. Jonah knew he had to make a command decision, but he just couldn't see any option that wouldn't put him right in the middle of several of them.

"Think, think, think, Jonah," he said to himself, almost softly enough to be a mere thought.

Nothing came to him, and he was one who knew how to get out of trouble. He'd been in plenty of bad spots as a Squad Leader during his military service. He'd led his two fireteams in three different deployments and had been involved in numerous incursions and firefights; more than he'd care to count, and he'd never lost a single man. But he was brain-locked on this one... He'd never seen an enemy combatant like this before, with no apparent concern for its own safety.

His phone rang loudly from his pocket, and Jonah almost crapped himself. He frantically reached for it to silence the ringing. It seemed to take forever to get his hand into his pocket and then to press one of its buttons to stop the incessant noise. He instantly remembered his scheduled alarm and cursed himself for not thinking to cancel it before it went off. He'd been called in the middle of the night to go to work and had forgotten all about it. Well, it was 5:00 AM and several of the nearest stinkers were shuffling directly toward Jonah. He nervously laughed at that thought, *stinkers*... He finally silenced the alarm.

While laying there, he had been watching them and studying their behavior and patterns, looking at how they moved, their speed, and trying to decipher their intent. He didn't see any. They were slow, and they moved weirdly, kind of jerky and mechanically, and they didn't seem to have any direction. It was as if they were waiting for something, but what? Then he realized he already knew the answer.

"Time to go," he said to himself, and he pushed up off the ground and began running as hard and as fast as he could. He knew precisely where his truck was and aimed right for it. Jonah kept his Sig M17 under his dash, and his Springfield Saint AR-10 pistol stashed in a secret compartment he'd built into his backseat. He'd feel a lot better if he could get to that truck. He conceal-carried his handgun into work for months, and had gotten away with it, until one day, Ted saw it as he reached up to get a cup to make his coffee in the small kitchen. Jonah never forgot the stupid look on Ted's smug face when he spotted it. It was almost comical, like an overly dramatic feigned shock. Jonah sighed and hurriedly pulled his sweater back down over his waistband to hide it, as if that would undo what had just happened. Ted made Jonah promise to never carry it again into the office and threatened to have Jonah fired if he ever suspected he did. Kraft had a very strict no-carry policy at work, and firearms were not permitted. On top of that, Ted was very anti-gun and Jonah was surprised he didn't turn him in. Ted had no idea what Jonah had been through or what it took to protect their way of life. Jonah blushed a bit from embarrassment and promised Ted he'd never do it again. It was hard for Jonah because he always had his pistol tucked into his waistband. He felt naked without it. But from that day on, he kept telling himself that it was only while he was in the office, and if he really needed it, he could get to it. That's when he started hiding it in his truck. Jonah had to get to his truck! He knew that his life depended on it.

Almost in unison, like a flock of birds, the freaks turned toward him. They all began their lumbering shuffle towards their prey, but Jonah was too fast, and they were too spread out. That didn't last long, however, because as he got closer to his truck, they got closer to him, almost as if they were funneling right toward it. It was just an illusion of their movement, but his window to get there was definitely closing fast. He'd sprinted his way past dozens, and knocked over two or three that he couldn't skirt around, but as he got closer to his truck, the horde squeezed in tighter and tighter.

With only 50 meters to go, Jonah knew he wouldn't make it. He could see his truck, but he would be surrounded by fifty of these things if he kept on his current trajectory. Jonah thought fast and led them away from his truck, and then somehow would try to double back to it. Making a ninety-degree turn in the building's direction, Jonah realized his fatal mistake almost as soon as he made it. The opening behind Jonah closed up with twenty meatheads, and several more were coming from the right. Then he saw fifteen more coming from the way he'd originally come, on the left. The stinkers who had chased him from behind had finally caught up to him and now he was flanked on both sides, as well as having a large group of them behind him. The building was straight ahead, but the entrance was on the other side of the right flanking group. There was no way to reach it without plowing through them, but there were far too many of them, and he knew he wouldn't make it. Jonah reached the building, but the deadheads cornered him, with no way out. Panting for breath, and heart racing, for the first time in his life, Jonah was certain he wasn't going to make it. His lower lip quivered a bit, then he steeled himself for what he was about to do.

A shot rang out, and in that instant, time stopped. Jonah dropped to the ground. The *deadheads*. Yeah, Jonah liked that one best, so that's what he'd call them from now on. They all stopped too. Then another shot pierced the early morning darkness, then another... He began scanning to see where it was coming from. He trained for this and identified the muzzle flash on the next round that was fired. It was coming from the roof of the two story building perpendicular to the one behind him, on the east side of the parking lot where he had parked his truck. Jonah couldn't see what the shooter was targeting, though. It was still very dark outside, and if he hit anything, or anyone, Jonah couldn't tell.

"Eddy? It has to be *Crazy Eddy*, that nutty security guard!" Jonah muttered to himself, and then smiled when he heard that idiot yelling at the top of his lungs to get the deadheads' attention.

"Over here, you stinky bastards, over here!" Eddy yelled with a voice that cracked like a teenaged boy who'd just hit puberty.

Eddy had always tried to act cool around Jonah, and had some strange man-crush on Jonah because he knew he had been in the military. Eddy said something about trying to serve, but couldn't pass the physical because of his asthma or some such nonsense. Mick, an E-4 on one of Jonah's fireteams, had asthma, and was one of the most badass soldiers Jonah had ever met. He knew Eddy was full of it, but he was always nice to him and never let on that he felt that way. After all, Jonah knew first hand that military service wasn't for everyone. But here he was now, that glorious goofy security guard, in the most dire situation Jonah had ever been in, and he was saving Jonah's butt.

A noticeably larger number of the deadheads on the right side of Jonah, the ones closest to the building Eddy was firing from, turned, and began their awkward shuffle toward him. While Eddy continued yelling, Jonah didn't waste a single moment of this precious life-saving time that Eddy had given him. He bolted up from the ground and assessed his opening, and determined the best path to get to his truck. He'd still need to push through a few of the deadheads, but only a few. Jonah liked his odds a lot better now.

As Jonah ran hard again, he continued hearing the shots fired from Eddy's location. It was definitely a high-powered rifle of some sort, a .308 or a .30–06, from the sound that cracked through the air with each round. Then, not 20 meters in front of Jonah, one dead-head fell to the ground as its head exploded like a rotten melon. Then another fell in almost the same manner. Eddy was an excellent shot for a rent-a-cop, and he most definitely had some sort of optic on that rifle of his, because he was at least 150 meters away. After each shot, Jonah heard Eddy yell something vulgar and ridiculous. It didn't bother Jonah one bit, though, and he was thankful for the help. Eddy was clearing the way for him. There was no doubt of that now, as all but a half dozen deadheads remained between Jonah and his truck.

Jonah was almost home free, with just 30 meters to go, and he had a clear line of sight all the way there. He wanted to yell something up to Eddy in thanks, but decided that a wave of his arm would have to do because Jonah didn't want to draw any more attention to himself. Jonah saw Eddy wave back at him, and that was good enough for him. Eddy was Jonah's hero for the moment and if he ever saw him again, he'd buy him a beer!

As Jonah reached for his keys, he scanned left, and then right, to be sure he was clear to proceed. He saw nothing that posed an immediate threat, although there were perhaps a hundred of the meatheads shambling his way from the direction he had come. He approached the door and punched the key-fob button to unlock his big 4x4, and he heard Eddy screaming something in his squeaky voice that he couldn't make out. Just as Jonah opened the driver-side door and lifted his left leg to get in, the open door slammed into him from behind with brutal impact. Jonah's right leg, now pinned outside the door, felt as if his shin bone had been broken. Searing pain shot through him. Stunned, Jonah tried to get the rest of the way in, but whatever was pressing against his door continued to do so, and his leg pinned there was in agonizing pain. The pressure wasn't constant, though; it pulsed in and out as if the thing were trying to crush him to death with his door. Then, something grabbed his leg just above the ankle; bony fingers wrapped around it like a clamp. And then Jonah just lost it. He screamed in pure rage and pushed back on the door with all his might. Whatever it was gave way, and Jonah could now put his left leg down on the ground. As he did so, he reached under his dash and grabbed his Sig P320, dropped the safety, and swung around in one fluid motion. The first of the two deadheads was just regaining his balance after being pushed back by the truck's door, and was lunging toward Jonah. As Jonah spun around, he quickly acquired his target and squeezed off three rounds of hollow point ammo in rapid succession, two to the chest, and one to the brain box, just as he had trained to do as an Army Ranger. Jonah was a skilled marksman, and the meathead dropped like a... well, like a sack of meat. He heard Eddy shout out some vulgar cheer as he adjusted his aim to target the second deadhead. Jonah then witnessed the most gruesome sight he'd ever seen. The deadhead was missing the entire left side of its face and nothing but jawbone and teeth were showing, but the weirdest part was that its mouth was working open and closed, over and over again. The thing was covered in a black ooze that smelled like a bucket of rotten fish that had sat in the sun for a couple of days. It was missing one eye, and the remaining eye was solid black. It was dawn now, and the light was just overtaking the night. Jonah had seen enough. He quickly punched two rounds into the thing's chest, but other than the impact pushing the thing back a couple of feet, it didn't seem to be bothered at all. He just regained his balance and started coming at Jonah again. Jonah stared in disbelief for a long moment, mesmerized by what he was witnessing. He already had the thing's forehead in his sights and he squeezed the trigger one more time. The disgusting thing's head exploded in a cloud of brain matter and black mist. Jonah heaved, and hurled right there on the spot. He couldn't help it. The sight and smell were more than he could handle, so there it was...

Jonah knew he had to compose himself, puking or not, and he needed to move *NOW*! He never saw those two coming, and there could be more in range and on him before he could get into his truck. He was in his truck within 10 seconds and pushing the button to start it up. The beast of a truck roared to life, and Jonah punched the accelerator and tore out of there like a cat with its tail on fire!

Chapter 13

Jonah's Escape

* * *

The racing engine, Jonah's pounding heart, the throbbing pain in his leg, and the macabre sights and sounds all around him worked together to keep Jonah focussed. He knew his pain and fear would keep him alive. His first Squad Leader had taught him that, and it was true if you knew how to channel it. Jonah did.

As he drove, dodging all the madness in his path out of the parking lot, Jonah's brain was almost on autopilot - processing his next action and formulating a workable plan. He was mentally crossing off things that would either be too risky or that would be just plain stupid. Jonah would not do anything stupid. But he needed to get home if he could. He decided he needed to get his gear and then try to make his way to Luke's old house. That's what he'd do. They could figure this out together. He just hoped that Luke was okay and that he could get to him. Jonah didn't have anyone else. His step-dad had abandoned any sort of relationship with Jonah years ago when Jonah joined the Army and had become a Ranger, rather than joining the family window and siding business. And his mom had died in a terrible car accident when he was on his 2nd deployment. Losing their parents was something that Luke and he shared and it made their bond that much stronger.

Jonah switched off the headlights to minimize the attention he seemed to get from all the things shambling around. *Don't be stupid.* He was only a couple of miles from his apartment and he knew this area, and could navigate it easy enough without the lights. Jonah was glad his apartment was on the ground floor and that he could pull right up to his front door. He only hoped that he could get there and that he could get inside safely. Not knowing what to expect when he made it there, Jonah knew most of his immediate neighbors, and they were all pretty decent folks, and he took a little comfort in that. What he didn't know was that *none* of them were quite themselves any longer.

Jonah was still holding his Sig in his right hand as he made one frantic turn after another. He was finding it more and more difficult to steer the truck while holding it, so he placed it between his legs and just under his leg to keep it from moving. He wanted to be able to get to it quickly if he needed it. After dodging one particularly large deadhead and narrowly missing a wrecked car, he rounded a bend in the road only to find crashed vehicles littering the road and shoulder, many with headlights still turned on, and a few were smoking or burning. Jonah didn't see a single vehicle moving, nor did he see any people, or *once-people,* as he rounded that bend. Jonah, mesmerized by the scene before him, couldn't believe his eyes. He was just on a small two-lane Parkway that ran between the business park and several residential neighborhoods, but it looked like Armageddon. Then there was movement just up ahead on the right side of the road. Jonah could see an overturned Jeep about 30 meters ahead and two people were climbing out of the side window. Jonah thought they were both female because of the long hair he could make out from their silhouettes. One pulled the other out, and then frantically scrambled to solid ground. As he got closer, he could clearly see that it seemed to be a mother and daughter. One was quite a bit smaller than the other, and she grabbed the taller one's hand and started pulling her away from the crash. Jonah was now only 15 meters away, and then there was something else. An arm appeared over the front wheel of the overturned jeep from its hidden side, then a head and massive shoulders, as it pulled itself up. Closer now, only 10 meters away, and Jonah could see the massive creature shambling towards the two girls. He was moving fast, too fast. The two females were trying to run, but the taller one was limping badly and couldn't move fast enough as the smaller one pulled hard on her hand. Jonah slammed on the brakes and looked in all directions for any other movement. He didn't see any, so he took a chance and flipped on the light bar on the front of his truck. It produced a brilliant beam of light and it instantly turned everything in its path into bright daylight. The deadhead was a fat gruesome male that was split open on his left side, with black stringy guts hanging out. He shouldn't have been moving at all, but now he, *it,* was almost upon the two females, and the younger one, Jonah, could now see that she couldn't be more than 11 or 12, began screaming. It was that nightmare-filled, piercing scream he'd heard too many times in his military past. He threw open his truck door and rolled down the window. He knew he couldn't run, not with his bad leg, so he did the only thing he could think of, he yelled at the two to drop to the ground, and as he did so, he swung around and out of the truck, putting most of his weight on his good leg, and he leveled his Sig at the beast, using the open window frame as a brace for his hands and weapon. They didn't listen to him. And now the deadhead was within 10 feet of them. Jonah yelled again for the girls to drop to the ground so he could fire at the beast.

"Please, drop to the ground. I'm here to help you, and I have a gun. Please get down so I don't accidentally shoot you," Jonah pleaded with the girls. He could hear the taller one yelling at the young girl to run, as the younger one was pulling her by the hand as hard as she could. She didn't seem to be hurt like the taller one was. The girl screamed, "Mom, do what he says." And the young girl dropped to the ground, even though her mother was still holding onto her. But, Jonah just couldn't take the shot. It was too risky, even though the young girl did what he asked. The mother was still standing, and now the deadhead was on her. It let out a hideous roar and tackled her to the ground so fast that Jonah couldn't do anything to help. He heard the woman screaming beneath the giant blob, a terror filled scream, and then gurgling, and then just the sounds the hideous beast was making.

Jonah could see the young girl scrambling away frantically, still low to the ground, and she appeared to be in shock. No sounds, just frantic and hitched breathing.

"Run to me. I'm in pretty bad shape, so I can't come get you. Please run, now!" Jonah yelled, but the girl didn't seem to hear him. Jonah tried again, but with the same result. So he gritted his teeth and made his way toward the unreal scene before him. His leg was aching badly, but he found he could put some weight on it and didn't think that the deadhead had broken it. He limped as quickly as he could toward the girl, who was now cowering next to a small tree about 20 feet from the blob on top of her mother. The thing was making disgusting inhuman sounds as it appeared to be eating the woman. Jonah got within a few feet of it, and without hesitation, raised his Sig to the beast's head and pulled the trigger. The young girl screamed again, but at least there was no more sound or movement from the thing.

In his most gentle voice he could muster, Jonah said, "It's okay, it's dead. Please sweetheart, come with me. I'm sure more of those things are near and we need to get out of here now." She just looked at Jonah and continued to breathe erratically. Jonah looked around them. It was a quick look, but practiced and experienced. They looked to be alone for now, but he didn't think that would last more than a minute or two. He took a few more steps toward her.

"I'm Jonah. I used to be a soldier, and I promise you're safe with me. What's your name?" he whispered.

She looked up at him, and her breathing seemed to slow a bit.

"I'm ah, Ss... Sophia."

"Well, it's nice to meet you Sophia, I'm so very sorry about your mom, I am." Jonah felt so stupid saying it, but he needed her to understand that her mother was gone, so that he could get her moving. "I wanted to help her too, but I just didn't get here in time," Jonah added. "But now we need to leave here, right now, you and me. And we have little time. I'll keep you safe, I promise, but you need to get up and come with me. Will you do that for me, Sophia?"

Her bright green eyes never left Jonah's, and she pushed herself up off the ground, as she said almost inaudibly, "Yes." She didn't say anything else.

Jonah reached out his hand to her, and she took it. His leg was hurting him, but he didn't let it show. He enclosed her small hand within his and held it firmly, and began making his way back to the truck. Well, as quickly as he could, given his gimpy leg. He didn't speak, and neither did she. They just focused on closing the distance to the safety of the big truck.

Just a step away now, and Jonah was close enough to reach for the open door. As his fingertips grazed the cold steel of the handle, Sophia screamed in surprise and her small hand ripped from his grasp, and something violently knocked her to the ground. Jonah spun around to see a woman on top of Sophia, savagely trying to get her teeth into her flesh. For such a small girl, Sophia was strong, and she held the shoulders of the woman pressing down on her, with all of her might, to keep her from biting her. Then he heard Sophia yell, "Mama, no mama, please stop!" Recognition of the woman hit Jonah, but he didn't want to believe what he was seeing. *How could this be? It's just not possible. It was too fast. How could I have been so stupid to forget about her?*

Jarred back into the moment with another ear-piercing scream, Jonah witnessed the nightmarish creature that was once Sophia's mother, trying to eat her own daughter. Still not believing the unreal scene, Jonah reached down and grabbed the woman by her long blonde hair and, with some effort, pulled her off of Sophia and flung her sideways to the ground a few feet away from the terrified girl. Jonah aimed his Sig at the woman, when Sophia screamed at him, "No, stop, please don't shoot my mom!" The plea was so heartbreaking and surreal that Jonah hesitated. And in that brief moment, the woman was on him. She moved so fast that he couldn't react in time to prevent her from latching onto him. Like a rabid cat, she was hissing and clawing, and trying to bite at him with every motion she made. It was a single-mindedness that reminded him of an animal. As she relentlessly attacked him, Jonah lost his balance, and they went tumbling to the ground together in a heap. As he fell, he lost the grip on his pistol and he no longer had possession of it. Jonah was a powerful man, but this woman seemed to have superhuman strength and it was all he could do to keep her from sinking her teeth into his throat. Time stood still, and for a moment Jonah didn't know how he was going to get out of this. He kneed her and punched at her, but with his hurt leg and his awkward position on the ground, he was struggling. Jonah never studied Jujitsu in any of his combat training, but focused more on Judo, Muay Thai, and knife skills. He sure wished he had now though, because he was on the ground and in a fight for his life. He learned some effective clinching techniques in Muay Thai, but they didn't seem to phase this creature in the least. She was pressing in on him and was now within just a few inches of his face with her furiously snapping teeth. Jonah was losing the fight, but with a burst of adrenaline, he managed to shove her back, though she remained on top of him. *BOOM!* He heard a deafening explosion, and the woman's head burst into a red and black mist that covered his face and eyes. The struggle dazed him for a moment he and couldn't tell if he was hurt beyond his already injured leg. He wiped frantically at his eyes with both hands to clear enough goop away to open them. The young girl came into focus, then. She was on her knees, sitting on her heels, with Jonah's Sig held within both of her small hands. She was crying. Through the ringing in his ears, Jonah heard her say, "I'm so sorry mama, I'm so sorry..." As tears flowed in tiny rivers down her pale cheeks.

Chapter 14

Jonah and Sophia

* * *

Jonah was a well-trained combat soldier, and he knew better than to lose focus on his surroundings, particularly when a threat was near. Missing something, no matter how small, could be very costly. He wouldn't let it happen again.

He took in his surroundings, following the gunshot and Sophia's heartbreaking cries to her mom. Jonah spotted a small group of dead-heads about 50 meters away. They were closing the distance in their awkward shamble. *The noise must have attracted them,* he thought. Though he was sympathetic to Sophia's fragile mental state, there was no time to deal with that now. He sucked up the pain in his leg and moved quickly to her and took the gun, which she still held limply in her hands, tucked it in his waistband, and scooped her up as gently as he could and shoved her in the open driver's side door. She was as light as a cricket; he thought. Jonah took one last look before jumping in. They were now only 25 meters away. Not so gently, he rammed the truck into reverse and whipped the truck around to drive in the opposite direction, only to reveal an even larger group in his headlights.

"No!" He yelled, and slammed on the brakes. The heavily wooded roadway on both sides would make it nearly impossible to go off-road, so he had to make a choice. He decided on the smaller group that he just turned away from. With a skillful three-point turn, Jonah pointed the big 4x4 directly at the smaller group, and stomped hard on the accelerator. The big throaty roar of the engine filled the early morning air, and Jonah didn't hesitate. He knew what he was going to do, and he was certain that it was his best option, given the situation.

The speedometer showed 51 miles per hour when he hit the first of the deadheads. It was one that had broken away from the others by a good 10-meter margin, and just before the big iron front bumper on Jonah's truck made impact, Jonah caught a fleeting glimpse of the inhuman face of the creature glowing in his headlights, but that was enough to burn the horrific image into his memory forever. The eyes were solid black, and half its face was just... just gone, with its teeth and jaw perfectly exposed. It looked like a piece of bloody meat was hanging from its mouth, but Jonah couldn't be sure about that, because a fraction of a second later, Sophia screamed loudly as it exploded in a gooey black mess that burst all over the windshield. And that was that. But then, just as quickly, the mass of what looked like at least a dozen more deadheads were now directly in the path of the 4-tons of Detroit steel, and Jonah knew it would not be pretty. "Hold on tight, Cricket," Jonah yelled.

It all happened so fast; in not much more time than it takes to blink twice, really. Even so, in that time, everything slowed, and felt to Jonah like long minutes instead. The beast of a truck made impact and their seatbelts tightened across them hard as the truck violently lost speed from plowing into the rotten mass of bodies. Then, except for the glow of the dashboard, there was darkness as the headlights and windshield smeared black from the mass. The truck bounced hard several times, and Jonah hit his head on the roof of the cab as the truck's tires rolled over the pile they had just mowed down. But he and Sophia held on tight. And then, just as fast as it came, it was over, as the truck fishtailed on the now smooth asphalt under them. Jonah quickly regained control as they picked up speed and left the nightmare behind them.

"You okay, Cricket?" Jonah huffed out.

"My name is Sophia," was all she said. Her voice was so low that it was almost inaudible. And she said nothing else.

"Well Sophia, I think we're okay now," he glanced over at her. But her face was expressionless as she stared blankly out the window.

Jonah focused on the road ahead. He didn't know what to do with her. He hoped her father, or grandparents, or family of some kind lived nearby. But then he realized that there was probably nowhere safe that he *could* take her, not with what's going on out there.

"Sophia, I don't know where to take you. Is your father, or another relative nearby?" Jonah asked. But Sophia continued her silence and didn't utter a sound. She just kept staring out the window. Jonah cleared his throat and tried again. "I need to get you somewhere safe, but I don't know where you live. Is there a place you'd like to go? Your dad maybe?" Jonah inquired. "I can take you there," he added. But there was nothing, no reaction, no reply, nothing. Jonah decided to just leave her alone for now. *Just let her try to process some of what'd happened,* he thought, as he realized she was probably in a mild state of shock. Jonah believed she would be okay, but as soon as he thought about it, he realized nothing would be okay. How could it be?

He gently reached over and touched the back of his hand to her tear-stained cheek, and let it linger there for just a moment as he tried to decide what to do next. Jonah's heart broke for the little girl. She was so small and seemed so fragile. And perhaps now, and tragically so, all alone in the world. Jonah was suddenly aware of an overwhelming need to protect her. At first he didn't understand the sudden and intense feeling, but then it all just sort of clicked together, like snapping the last piece of a puzzle into place to complete a beautiful picture. Hadn't that been his purpose all along?

The thing that compelled him to become a soldier? He was a protector, and he had always been driven... no, it was even stronger than that. In his very essence, he needed to guard and to protect; particularly the small, and the weak, who couldn't protect themselves.

Jonah thought about little geeky Bobby Anderson from Junior High. Bobby was a painfully shy and rail-thin boy who was in Jonah's 6th grade class. He never paid much attention to Bobby until one day in the cafeteria, when the Junior High bully, Peter Rollins, tripped Bobby as he was walking to his seat with his lunch tray. Jonah had been sitting with his friends at the "jock" table, cracking jokes, and sneaking glances at the cute girls sitting at the cheerleader table, when suddenly, Bobby went face first to the floor, landing in such a way that his Frito pie and chocolate pudding wound up all over his face and in his hair. Jonah saw the whole thing, including the foot that purposely shot out at just the right moment to send Bobby sprawling to the floor. Jonah had run-ins with Pete before, and Pete typically avoided Jonah, even though Pete had a good 15 pounds on Jonah. But Jonah was on the football team and fairly popular. Bullies usually avoided the popular kids. They seemed to prefer the kids who didn't *fit in* somehow. Pete was big for a Junior High kid, and it was rumored that he had been held back a couple of times before he moved to Mason City two years ago with his dad, who was a diesel mechanic at a local garage, but no one knew for sure. Pete always hung out with Clay Lozinski, another Junior High troublemaker.

Jonah got up and helped Bobby back to his feet, and gathered all the napkins from his table and gave them to Bobby to help him get cleaned up some.

"Hey man, you okay?" Jonah asked.

Bobby gave Jonah a weak smile, and said, "Yeah, thanks."

"You sure?" Jonah really felt sorry for Bobby.

"Yeah, I'm sure."

"You better go to the bathroom and use some water to help get some of that off."

"Okay," was all Bobby said as he turned in total embarrassment, and began walking quickly towards the hallway where the boys' bathroom was located. As he walked away, he could hear Pete and Clay laughing and saying ugly words about him, thinking he couldn't hear what they were saying. He could.

Jonah glared at Pete for a long moment, seething inside. Then, without a word, he reached down to his table and grabbed his own tray loaded with french fries, ketchup, half a burger, and a half-full carton of chocolate milk, and walked right up to Pete and dumped the entire tray right into his lap. For a long moment, Pete just looked up a Jonah, dumbstruck, but then rage festered in his eyes, and faster than a kid his size should've been able to move, Pete was on top of Jonah, and began whaling away at his face with his fists. Before Jonah knew what happened, his entire table of jock friends were pulling Pete off him. It was then that the Principal, Mr. Matthews, seemed to appear out of thin air and stood over Jonah. Jonah watched from the floor as Mr. Matthews, with expert eyes, assessed the situation, and he seemed to understand exactly what had happened without saying a single word. Mr. Matthews held out his hand and helped Jonah to his feet.

"You alright son?" he asked Jonah.

"Yes sir," Jonah replied politely, as he wiped blood from his nose.

Mr. Matthews then glared at Pete, who stood there with a stupid smirk on his face. "Peter Rollins, my office, now!" he commanded. Then he looked at Jonah sympathetically and said, "You too, Jonah."

"But..." Jonah started, but was interrupted.

"No buts. Fighting is against school rules. Now get moving," Mr. Matthews ordered, but with a tinge of sympathy in his voice.

As it turned out, Jonah got detention for a week after school, but they suspended Peter for the same time period. When Pete came back to school the following week, he had a good-sized bruise on his cheekbone, and the underside of his eye was a little black and blue too. Jonah heard a few days later that Pete got a pretty good beating from his father. He hoped that was true. Jonah despised bullies.

He would protect Sophia, he would protect her with his life.

Jonah was pulled out of his thoughts when Sophia said unexpectedly, "What kind of gun is that?" as she pointed to his lap where he held his Sig.

Without missing a beat, Jonah said, "Army calls it a M17, it's a Sig P320." He wanted to sound relaxed because he knew what a fragile state Sophia was in.

"You're a soldier?"

Jonah was surprised at how calm she sounded, and her voice was strong and matter of fact.

"I was, but not anymore."

"Will you teach me?" she surprised Jonah.

Jonah glanced over at her. "Teach you what?"

"Teach me how to shoot it."

Jonah didn't answer right away. He thought about all that had happened in the past hour, and about how she had really saved him. *Damn, she really did save my butt. There are plenty of grown men who would have froze-up in a situation like that.*

"Yes," was all he said.

Sophia didn't say anything else either, but looked ahead through the windshield again.

Jonah continued slowly on the deserted country parkway as he headed toward his apartment, which was only a mile away now. He pulled over to the side of the road and killed the engine. It was light outside now and there wasn't another person in sight. *Or deadhead,* he thought. He watched carefully through the windshield for a minute, then turned to look behind them. As he studied their surroundings, he heard Sophia shuffle in her seat. He turned and looked at her. She was sitting Indian style, again looking so small. She was staring right at him. He wondered if he could still sit that way and couldn't remember the last time he'd even tried.

"You know Cricket, we have to make a tough decision."

"Why do you keep calling me that?" she snapped.

"I don't know. Look at you," he smiled. "You're small like a cricket and, well, sort of bendy like a cricket. You just remind me of one, that's all," Jonah said with a hint of a smile.

"Well, I don't like it," she said. "Why have we stopped?"

"I need to decide where we should go next. My first plan was to go to my apartment and get some of my supplies. It's close by, but the more I think about it, the more I think it may be a bad idea."

"Why?"

"Too populated there. I'm thinking that's not a good thing right now."

"You know, you're pretty smart for a soldier," she said with a straight face.

"Thanks," Jonah said, and gave her a small wink.

"So what do we do, then?" she asked.

"Well, I've been thinking about that. I know of a small gun shop not too far from here. It's kind of hidden out of the way and in a quiet neighborhood. I buy supplies there sometimes. In the Army, they teach you about the important things you should do first in dangerous situations. Security is at the top of the list."

"Is that like safety?" she asked.

"In a way, yes. You see, when bad things are happening around you, the most important thing you have to do first is to protect yourself and those around you from harm. Then, shelter is next, followed by water and food. Those are the things you need to survive," Jonah said. "The protection part is security," he added.

"You have a gun. That counts, right?"

"Yes Cricket!" But before she could speak, he corrected himself, "Sorry, Sophia."

She just glared at him, but then asked, "But it's not enough, is it?".

"Hey, you're pretty smart for a little girl."

She remained expressionless at his attempt to make her smile. "There are a lot of those things out there. One gun isn't enough. I know it isn't."

"No, it isn't Sophia. I've got another gun in the truck, and a small amount of ammunition, but it's not going to be enough to keep us safe for very long." Jonah paused for a moment. "Especially if we run in to a large group of them," he finished.

"Thank you for trying to help me and my..." Sophia's breath caught in her throat. "My mom," she finished. "What's happening to all these people, Jonah?"

"I'm not sure exactly, but I have a feeling it's kind of like a very contagious virus. Something really bad that they transmit to each other through biting. Kind of like rabies in some dogs and other wild animals. Do you know what that is?"

"Yes, I know what that is. I'm not stupid!"

"Sophia, can I tell you something?"

"You just did." she turned her head away from him so he couldn't see, and smiled to herself.

"Well, I've never really been around kids before, so I'm gonna say the wrong thing sometimes. Sophia, believe me when I say - I know you're not stupid. You handled yourself like a real combat soldier back there. You have great natural instincts."

It was quiet for a few moments, when Jonah decided to get moving, and started up the truck. He knew some back roads to get to the McKenzie Brothers gun shop. It was about five miles from their current location. He just hoped he could get them there safely and that they could get inside.

"Can I have your extra gun?" Sophia broke the silence.

"Sophia, I'll teach you, I promise. Just as soon as we are some-place safe and we have some time to work on it. But you have to trust me on this. Guns are extremely dangerous, and we're going to do this my way, okay? I've seen some firearms accidents up close over the years, and believe me, you never want anything like that to happen to you. Or to me, for that matter. Deal?"

"Okay, deal," Sophia said, disappointed.

"I'm not going to let anything happen to you, Sophia. I give you my word. I'm a soldier, remember?"

Sophia stared at him for a moment, but when he turned his eyes from the road for a moment and looked back at her, and caught her staring at him, she just rolled her eyes.

"I saw that," Jonah said. "How old are you, anyway? 10? 11?"

"I'm 13!" she snapped.

"Sorry, it's just you're kinda—"

"Small! I know, I hear that all the time."

"Like I said, I've never been around kids before. Well, not since I was one, anyway."

"Well, I am small for my age. Mom said I haven't hit my growth spurt yet. I'm still waiting for that."

Jonah couldn't help but smile at the levity of the conversation. It was a pleasant distraction.

Driving slowly along River Heights Drive, Jonah kept his eyes sharp. It was a heavily wooded residential area, and though the homes were built in the 50s, they were well maintained, giving the neighborhood a quaint, old-fashioned feel. The sun was just above the horizon, so the neighborhood was still quite dark beneath the canopy of large maple, oak, and elm trees. He had to maneuver around a few cars and trucks that appeared to be left abandoned in the middle of the road, or halfway into or out of driveways. Some had their doors opened, and he half expected to see people getting out of them. But there wasn't a soul in sight. As he drove particularly close to one car, a Suburban, to get around it because it sat in the middle of the road, he could make out what looked like a large smear of blood on the driver's side window, and an even larger pool of blood on the ground just beneath the opened door. As Jonah focussed on their surroundings, he made out movement within the deep blues and grays between the houses and trees. It didn't feel right at all though, and his heart beat just a little faster. Warning bells began to ring in his brain, telling him to get out of there. On a normal day, he would expect to see cars backing out of driveways as folks were leaving for work, or taking their kids to school, or walking their dogs. But there were no cars moving, no moms rushing their kids out of their front doors while trying to adjust their backpacks hanging haphazardly off their shoulders, or shoving lunch bags into their hands. There were no joggers or dogs on leashes. There was nothing. Nothing except for the occasional flicker of movement that was always just out of sight, and what looked like piles of laundry on the ground, spattered about here and there. It didn't take Jonah long to figure out what those piles of laundry really were, but he didn't say anything because he didn't want to frighten Sophia. She hadn't seemed to put two and two together yet.

As Jonah began to make out the silhouettes of the twin steeples of the beautiful 120-year-old St Joseph's Catholic Church, he noticed the Church grounds and intersecting road ahead were blotted out grey somehow, and they seemed to move, almost like a big dark wave. Was it an optical illusion, like when you drive on a long highway on a hot, sunny day, and see ripples and waves? He couldn't make sense of it. And then he did. There must have been a thousand of them, gruesome and thick, shoulder to shoulder and front to back, moving in unison right toward them, blocking any path forward.

Chapter 15

Ma Deuce

* * *

At the sight of the horde of meatheads shambling directly toward them, Jonah's mouth fell open in total disbelief as he hit the brake pedal hard, instinctively throwing his right arm out to hold Sophia in her seat. She only had the lower part of her seatbelt secured, and the shoulder strap was behind her, a habit she had gotten into riding with her mom, because the belt would rub against her cheek and neck. She threw her hands out in front of her and said, "What is it?"

"You don't see that?" Jonah continued, staring in disbelief.

Sophia squinted, "Is that—"

"Yeah, and we need to get out of here fast! Hold on!"

Jonah turned the wheel hard left and drove over the curb and directly into the grass of the closest yard. The truck fishtailed as it threw up grass, rocks, and dirt, and he thought even a mailbox. Sophia grabbed the handle above her door and held on tight. As the truck straightened and made it back onto the road, a woman and two teenaged boys unexpectedly appeared directly in front of them, running toward the truck from the other direction. They were yelling something that Jonah couldn't make out, but he knew it was a cry for help. There was something else, though. Shadowy figures shuffled out from between the trees and shadows of the houses all around them, and they were clearly targeting the trio of survivors.

Now becoming routine, Jonah hit the brakes again, but Sophia prepared this time and braced herself. "Stay here, don't open your door," and he jumped out of the truck and yelled to the woman and two boys, "Run! Hurry! Don't look back, just run to me!" He could hardly hear himself over the stadium-like roar of moans coming from behind him, and then the smell hit him. It was the concentrated stench of a thousand rotting corpses assaulting him all at once, poisoning the air around them. It was so thick that he could taste it, and he gagged. The woman and two boys were about 30 meters away, when the tallest of the two boys tripped and went sprawling to the ground. Jonah could see several of the figures immediately zero in on him and move toward the boy in a frenzy.

It was in that half-second, in that brief flicker of time, there in that tiny little place within the expanse and vastness of God's infinite universe, that a million things unfolded all at once. And none of them were good.

Sophia screamed, "Jonah, no, don't leave me, please come back! You promised to keep me safe!"

As the boy tried to get to his feet, the fastest of the grotesque figures tackled him back to the ground, and the boy screamed the most horrific sound that Jonah had ever heard. At the sound of the boy's tormented scream, the woman turned and wailed, "Baby, no, baby, Mama's coming!" Without hesitation, the woman changed direction and ran back to her son. Two more deadheads were only a few feet away from the boy, who was still screaming in agony and hysterically wrestling with the creature on top of him. Jonah took a knee, raised his Sig and let fly three quick shots that downed one of the approaching deadheads. He had no shot at all at the one on top of the boy. With the first one down, he turned slightly and took aim at the second one, but before he could squeeze the trigger, the woman moved in front of his sights, and then it was just too late. The second deadhead was on top of her, and after only a muffled scream, had her throat out and between his teeth. The smaller boy was crying uncontrollably, breath convulsing, as he turned to help his mother. He began punching at the thing, trying to get it off her. There was nothing Jonah could do. Frozen and unable to help these poor souls, Jonah watched in horror. The screams coming from the boys were unbearable and tore at his heart. Even before Jonah could get to his feet, five more were on top of the second boy and his mother. The sight was more than he could bear. He stood and began unloading his Sig into the creatures in rapid fire succession, expertly changing targets after two shots each. But there were just too many of them, and they just kept coming. It only took a few brief moments before the slide locked back on the Sig, signaling that it was empty.

As tears silently streamed down his cheeks, Jonah could hear Sophia pleading with him to get back into the truck.

"Jonah, hurry, we're not gonna make it. They're almost here!" she yelled, voice cracking, pleading with him to come back.

Jonah knew he had to move. His leg was still racked with pain, but he wasted no time in getting back to the truck as fast as he could. He didn't make it. From his blind left side, and slightly behind him, a powerful blow knocked him to the ground. Sophia screamed in surprise because even she hadn't seen the deadhead coming. He was big, almost as big as Jonah. The stink and cold of the thing was what Jonah noticed first. It was awful, like having a giant rotting piece of meat on top of him. But the thing was clumsy, and it had landed awkwardly on top of Jonah, sort of sideways, and it was flailing around, almost in slow-motion, trying to turn its face toward Jonah for a bite. Jonah rolled it off him in the moment or two he had been given. Then, in a blur, Jonah saw another figure running at him. He braced for another impact, but the figure stopped short of him, and with great speed, raised something long and pointy over its head with two small hands, and just as the first deadhead had managed to rollover onto its back, brought it down hard and sunk it deep into the creature's face. It stopped moving then. Jonah tried to wipe the putrid black goo from his forehead and eyes, and as he did, he realized it was Sophia. The girl was fast, lightning fast, and had saved Jonah for a second time. She had found his long Ranger's trench knife under the seat of the truck and used it to silence the deadhead.

"Get up, we're out of time, hurry Jonah, hurry, they're coming!"

Jonah grunted, got to his feet, and took her small hand as she pulled him to the truck. Surprised by how strong the little girl was, Jonah allowed her to lead him to the awaiting open door. She jumped in first and hopped over the cushioned center console, as Jonah got into his seat and slam the door shut. The cozy and warm interior of the cab was a stark contrast to the nightmare just outside their small sanctuary.

Jonah jammed the gear selector into drive as he glanced into the rearview mirror. His stomach went queazy at the sight of the endless grey sea of deadheads he saw there, and the first of them were already upon them, with their outstretched arms reaching for the tailgate of his truck. But in front of him were no less than 30 more gruesome figures coming straight at them from that direction. He could still see the worm-like writhing of the dozen or so gathered at the bodies of the mother and two teenage boys, their heads buried in the torsos in a macabre frenzy

"Hold on Cricket, this is gonna get bumpy!" He pressed down hard on the accelerator, but the truck didn't respond as he had expected. Instead, the truck seemed to bog down and the front of the truck began lifting upward. As Jonah realized what was happening, Sophia looked behind them through the back glass and let out a sharp scream that filled the small space within the truck's cab. He didn't know how many, more than he thought possible, and the back of the truck spilled over with a writhing pile of ghastly figures that were once just ordinary folks, like him and Sophia. And more were clawing their way over the top of *them*. From the front of the vehicle, a deadhead had jumped onto the hood and was pressing its inhuman face into the windshield. When Sophia turned back to face forward, an even louder scream escaped her as the gnashing teeth of the near faceless beast were biting and breaking off as it tried to bite Sophia through the glass. Greasy black ooze smearing the thin barrier between them.

Jonah's heart was racing as he tried again and again to pull away from the massive horde closing in on them from behind, but the truck couldn't gain any traction and the rear wheels just spun in place, or maybe they weren't turning at all, as the truck simply would not move.

"Sophia, open the glove box and get the two mags for the Sig in there."

"What?" she cried, "I don't understand!"

Jonah clarified, as he place the truck into four-wheel drive and rammed the gear in to low, "Bullets, the magazines for my handgun!" Sophia opened the door of the glove box and saw what must have been the things Jonah was asking for. She grabbed the two metal bullet holders that he needed. In less than two seconds, Jonah had dropped the magazine that was in the Sig and shot his hand out to Sophia. She put one of the magazines in his hand and he rammed it home. The slide shot forward, forcing a round into the chamber. He pressed the gun into her hand. "Don't point it at me or you and don't put your finger on the trigger unless you are going to pull it!" he commanded. "Hold it with two hands and if anything comes through the windows, shoot it!" he added. Sophia took the P320 and gripped it in her hands as she pointed it to the windshield.

He hit the accelerator hard once more, and the big diesel roared as the truck lurched forward. Jonah had the accelerator all the way to the floor. The engine screamed and the truck gained a little ground. First a foot, then two, then ten, and he rammed it into high gear and floored it again. They picked up speed, and Jonah could see they were leaving the larger group behind them. But the front of the truck was so high now that Jonah couldn't see where they were going. They hit another deadhead on the driver's side and it latched onto the outside mirror of the truck. Then Jonah got an idea. It was risky, but he had to do something or they were going to crash and that would be the end of them.

"Brace yourself, Cricket!" Jonah yelled, and he jerked the steering wheel hard to the left and intentionally hit an SUV sitting in the road on his side. The oily sludge of the deadhead that was holding onto the outside mirror, splattered all over the window as the impact crushed it between the two large vehicles. Just as quickly, Jonah turned hard to the right, all the while keeping the accelerator floored. As he did, his left shoulder hit the driver's side door hard from the inertia shift, and then he did the same thing again to the left. He tried to do it fast enough, hoping to keep the truck on the road. The gradual lowering of the front end of the truck, and a quick glance in the mirror, told him it was working. The deadheads were being tossed out of the bed of the truck like lifeless rag dolls. He continued this erratic left-to-right motion until the front of the truck lowered enough so that Jonah could see. But when he finally could see ahead, he almost wish he couldn't.

There were only a few clinging deadheads remaining in the truck's bed but they were struggling to gain any sort of balance, and Jonah swore he could see several detached arms still hanging from the sides and tailgate of the truck with their clinched hands and fingers holding fast. The horde behind them was now about thirty meters back, but the road ahead of them was also blotted out by another large group approaching from the front. It was a nightmare scenario, and Jonah couldn't see any way out. There were far too many in either direction to drive through them. It was like watching an ominous tidal wave approaching, and knowing there was no way to outrun it.

Jonah stopped the truck and turned his head to the rear for a quick glance back, and the majestic twin steeples that topped the ornate red-brick Catholic Church were now in full sunlight. They were beautiful with the bright morning sky behind them, and for a moment, the sight comforted Jonah. But the roiling grey mass beneath them stole that away just as quickly. He reached for Sophia's hand. She gave it to him, sobbing and trembling. Before Jonah could say a word, an enormous red Hummer pickup truck came roaring from between two of the houses on the right, and plowed into the mass of bodies in front of them, making a formidable hole in the group, but not enough for Jonah to hope to squeeze through. Jonah had seen this Hummer before, in the parking lot of the Plant where he worked. He didn't know who owned it, but it was there in the parking lot almost every day. It was a beast of a truck with a big lift, monster tires, and gadgets galore. The behemoth sat there idling, unmoving, with windows tinted so black that Jonah could not see inside them. There were body parts strewn in every direction from the impact, many missing limbs still clambering along, and Jonah even saw one missing everything below the waist, pulling itself along in a sickening effort to reach it. But there were still too many of them, and within moments, they had the Hummer surrounded.

To Jonahs's and Sophia's surprise, a man popped up in the bed of the Hummer pickup, pulling the tarp off something mounted in the back of the tall truck.

"No! That's impossible!" Jonah said almost involuntarily. "That's a Ma Deuce!" Then he let out a low whistle. "An honest to goodness Ma Deuce!" he repeated.

"What's a ma da... dose?" Sophia asked, struggling to pronounce the second word.

"Well Cricket, it's a really bad day for anything unfortunate enough to be in front of it."

Just as Jonah finished his sentence, the big twin-handled M2 .50 caliber machine gun rattled to life, spitting out its enormous rounds in long bursts, cutting everything down in its path. Chunks of meat, bone, dirt, and black mist filled the air. Nothing in its wake escaped its awesome destruction. It was an absolute bone-chilling sight to witness.

"That crazy son of a..." Jonah said, in awe of the scene before him. The entire mass of deadheads behind the Hummer was just gone. Erased! And Jonah didn't waste a single moment putting the truck in gear and flooring it, to hightail it out of there before that giant hole closed up. As Jonah got closer to the Hummer, the figure manning the turret-mounted machine gun swung the Ma Deuce around to face the horde closing in on the right side, and Jonah could see his face clearly.

"Crazy Eddy, God bless you, man! Now get out of here!" Jonah yelled out the window that he managed to roll down just a little as he drove by. Eddy looked at Jonah and just smiled his big, goofy smile. Then he took his right hand off the big gun for a moment, stood tall, and saluted Jonah. Crazy Eddy then turned and went back to work, mowing down the horde. Jonah could swear that Eddy was actually happy.

Once Jonah and Sophia were in the clear and a good 100 meters away from the mob of rotting creatures, he stopped and looked back to see if Eddy had made it out of there. But he could hear it much easier than he could see it. That crazy Eddy was still shredding the meatheads in a 180 degree arc around the front of the Hummer. Jonah couldn't help but to be mesmerized by the sight. Sophia stood on the seat and popped her head out of the sunroof of the truck to watch, too. She had never seen anything like it, not even in the movies. The larger group had closed the distance now, and even though the Ma Deuce was performing admirably, there were just too many of them. They were closing in around the arc of the fire path. Jonah got a sick feeling in his gut. He reached into the center console and took out a pair of binoculars to get a closer look. It only took a quick glance through the glasses for Jonah to see the swarm encircle the giant Hummer. And though it appeared too high for them to reach Crazy Eddy, they once again clambered over one another, using the slower and weaker ones as steps to get higher and higher. Jonah knew what was about to happen, and he didn't want Sophia to see it. He jumped back in and pulled her hand to get her back down in her seat. He saw she was still holding the Sig in her left hand, and he watched it carefully as she climbed down from the console and took her seat. She was very careful of the powerful handgun and where she pointed the muzzle. She seemed to understand the importance of that. "Why did you pull me back in? I wanted to watch him kill those monsters," she huffed.

"We have to go Sophia. We almost didn't make it out of there. Let's try to get to the gun shop if we can. I'm sure we'll be safe there until we figure out what we're going to do next," Jonah said. "Hey, I want you to hold on to that for me," he said, pointing to his pistol. "But I want you to hold it flat in your palm for a moment. I need to do something."

She held it flat in her hand as she moved it toward Jonah. He reached over and clicked on the safety.

"There, that's called the safety. You can't fire the gun when the lever is up like that. I'll teach you more later, okay?" he said with a hint of a smile.

"Okay," Sophia replied softly.

"What do you say we get outta here now?"

"Yes, it stinks bad here," Sophia replied, scrunching up her nose.

Jonah did the same, and said, "Man, it sure does." Then he put the truck in gear and drove away.

Chapter 16

Refuge

* * *

Luke awoke to Archie licking his face. As he opened his eyes, he was immediately aware of how dark it was. "Great, still in the dark," he mumbled. The candle had long since burned itself out, and Grandpa's basement had no windows, and so to Luke, the time of day remained a mystery. "How long was I asleep, boy?" he absently asked Archie, but Archie just continued licking Luke's face. Archie was on the other side of Luke now, and without thinking about it, Luke lifted his right hand to rub Archie's head and was painfully reminded of his injured shoulder. But he noticed it didn't hurt nearly as much. The gash and the sore bone beneath stung as he moved it, but it wasn't at all like last night, or whatever time it was when he cleaned it up and bandaged it.

Luke pushed himself up into a sitting position. The basement was chilly, and he still didn't have a shirt on. He needed to find some clothes to wear. His stomach rumbled loudly... And something to eat.

"Okay, first things first," he said aloud. Then he stood up, using the toilet to help lift himself up, and he reached over to the countertop for his flashlight and clicked it on. Everything looked exactly the same as he had left it. He wasn't sure why he noticed that, but then he thought of all the crazy stuff that he and Archie had been through before finally making it down here into Grandpa's basement. He also realized how quiet it was now; there was no more banging and scratching on the door upstairs.

He ruffled Archie's head, and he could tell that his pooch needed to do his business. Luke hadn't thought about that yet. "Well, boy, let's see what we can figure out."

He carefully tried to put some weight on his aching right foot, and it surprised him he could at all. It hurt a lot, but he hobbled out the door and shone the flashlight around the main basement room. His gramps really had done a lot down here. There was even a full-size gas stove against the back left wall, with a vent hood that had a pipe leading up, then it bent at a 90-degree angle straight into the wall that Luke was certain led nowhere but into the earth that he knew was behind it. Well, at least that's what used to be there. To the left of the stove was a small countertop with a single drawer, and a host of knives and cutlery on the wall above that, held in place by some sort of magnet. Next to the stove on the right hung an array of pots and pans. And under those was a shelf with cases of canned food. He only knew that because he saw a big Campbell's soup label on the box; Chunky Steak and Potato. Luke's mouth watered, thinking about having some of that soup, but he first needed to figure out what to do about Archie's immediate problem. "I'll come back to you soon. Don't go anywhere, sweetheart," he winked at the soup. *Great, now I'm talking to soup...*

Luke shone the light around the room some more, and decided on one door that he noticed when they first made it down here, but had never seen before then. He began the slow limp in that direction. It hurt, but he was thankful just to use both feet again. Well, sort of. The door was on the far left wall, to the left of the stove, and when he got there, he leaned against it to rest for a moment. Archie began sniffing around the bottom of the door. "Well, let's see what's behind door number 1," Luke said playfully.

When he opened the door, a damp, musty smell came wafting out of the room. When he got his light in there and shone it around, he could see why. "Gramps, what have you been up to down here?" he whispered in disbelief. What Luke saw blew his mind. It was a new excavation. It was unfinished, but it was the makings of a large room, and it still had a dirt floor. There were several piles of dirt in various places, with the odds and ends of various construction debris piled in others. The walls were some sort of cinder block construction, and the ceiling had steel beams running in one direction, and just above them, thick wood beams running perpendicular. "How in the world..." Luke slowly trailed off.

Archie moved in quickly and started sniffing around hurriedly. Dirt was one thing Archie knew very well, and there was still plenty of it in this room. "It's okay, boy, this is as good of a place as any. Go ahead, do your thing," Luke said to his companion. Once done, Luke knew he'd have to bury that mess, but that would have to wait until he felt better. He noticed several tools leaning against the walls, including a couple of shovels. Luke called Archie back out the door, and he closed it behind them.

Luke made a B-Line for the stove, and to the soup that he could almost taste already. He hoped the stove worked, but even if it didn't, he'd just eat it right out of the can. He could remember doing that plenty of times before when camping or hunting. But man, how he hoped he could heat it up; it would taste so much better, hot. Besides, it was cold down here, and having something warm to eat would make him feel better.

The stove was only a few painful steps away. He put both hands on the front corners of the stove-top and then studied it with his flashlight for a moment. Then, he twisted one of the burner knobs on the front of the stove to see if it would light. It didn't. But he heard the hiss of gas coming out, and he bent over slightly to sniff it. It was definitely gas, but the igniter wasn't working. Luke decided that it probably needed electricity for that part to work, and he twisted it off. He looked around the stove top and small shelves near him for any matches. He didn't see any. "Well boy, looks like we're eating cold soup," he said to Archie. He just didn't have the strength or patience right now to hobble back to the bathroom to get matches or a lighter. He was hungry, and cold soup would be just fine.

Luke reached down to the top case. Thankfully, it was just below waist high, and he picked it up and sat it on top of the stove. He grabbed a knife from the magnetic holder on the wall and cut the box open with precision. Luke was a bit of a perfectionist and always did things carefully and methodically. After opening the box, he put the knife back on its holder, and then pulled out four cans of soup and lined them up in a neat row on the stovetop. Luke looked down at Archie, who was sitting right next to him, looking right back up at Luke with hopeful eyes. "You hungr—," he tried to say, but Archie cut him off with a loud bark. He knew Luke had food, and he wanted some as soon as possible.

Luke opened a can with the pull ring on top and removed the lid. With great care, he leaned over and set the open can down on the floor for Archie. He didn't know how comfortable it would be for Archie to eat out of the can, but Luke knew that he'd figure it out. Now it was Luke's turn. He looked around for a spoon but only found one of the large serving kind. He decided that he'd join Archie and just drink it right out of the can because that thing was too big to eat from. After they both finished a second can of soup, Luke lined the empty cans up again on top of the stove. He'd figure out what to do with them later. But right now, there were more important things to do, like finding some clothes to wear, and getting some light going in this dark basement. The cold soup didn't do a thing to warm him up, and he was tired of carrying a flashlight around, or worse, having no light at all.

Luke spent the next couple of hours exploring the basement and uncovering some of its many hidden treasures. One room was a bunk room, complete with 8 military style bunk beds, all made to perfection with crisp white sheets, and thick wool blankets. Luke shook his head at the thought of sleeping on the cold bathroom floor when this room was just 30 feet away. There were also two large metal dresser style cabinets filled with t-shirts, socks, underwear, sweatpants, shorts, and even a few pairs of long johns. In the room's corner was a large closet filled with cargo pants, jackets, coats, sweatshirts, hoodies, and several long-sleeved and short-sleeved shirts, all neatly hung. Luke also saw a rack of boots and tennis shoes in the back of the closet. But the best find to Luke was a multi-band radio, with a sort of wind-up generator handle on the side. Stamped Kaito KA900 on the front, it looked to be well made. Luke also found some old-fashioned oil lamps, with several jugs of paraffin oil.

Luke discovered that Gramps had installed some sort of ventilation system to pipe out stale air, and exhaust from the lamps and stove. He figured his grandpa had set it up to work with a natural vacuum of some kind, because there was no power on in the house, but it still circulated the air. His grandpa was a very smart man, and Luke had always admired him. *It's as if Gramps knew something was coming*, Luke thought. This was no half-hearted effort. Gramps filled the basement with enough supplies and emergency equipment to provide for several people for quite a long time. Luke never knew how serious his grandpa was about all this stuff.

There was still more to explore, but Luke decided it would have to wait. After what felt like two or three hours had passed, Luke was feeling fatigued. After all, he was pretty beat up, and his shoulder and ankle were really hurting him now.

Luke looked at himself in the bathroom mirror. He looked like crap and felt even worse, so he began the daunting task of taking a shower and brushing his teeth. He had brought a clean change of clothes with him into the bathroom. Though Gramps had stocked up on several sizes of clothes to prepare for whomever may join him down here, he and his gramps were the same height, and about the same build, so there was plenty for Luke to choose from. He grabbed a pair of OD green cargo pants and a long-sleeved black t-shirt. Luke also grabbed a pair of boxers and a pair of wool socks. Luke hated boxers, but it was all he could find in his quick search of the underwear drawer.

The shower was hot, and it felt beyond great. Luke could feel all the crud of the past... how long had it been? He didn't know, hours? Days now? It was all a big blur at this point, but it washed away. Luke wanted to stand in that shower forever, after being chased through the house by those stinking rotting things, and being beat all to crap. And to cap it all off, sleeping on the cold bathroom floor. After scrubbing himself down the best he could, he took another few moments to savor the hot water washing over him. He left his bandage on his shoulder to shield it from the water jetting out at him, and that seemed to work out, but he'd still need to re-dress that and wrap his ankle before heading back to the bunk room to lie down for a bit.

Luke didn't want to get out, but he knew he couldn't stay in there much longer. He was feeling fatigued from standing so long under the hot water, so he dried himself off and put on his boxers and pants. He hobbled over to the toilet and sat down there to change the bandage on his shoulder. When he peeled off the old bandage, the wound was still sealed up with the glue, and he thought it looked pretty good. As he put the new bandage on, there were four loud bangs coming from somewhere outside the door at the top of the stairs. It was loud enough to make Luke jump and Archie bark. The bangs were in quick succession, and for a moment, Luke thought they sounded like gunshots, and they were followed by what sounded like a muffled scream. "Easy boy," Luke said to Archie. Luke froze, listening for any further sounds, but there was nothing. He was shaking. The ordeal over the past... *how long had it been?* He didn't know, but it had caught up to him now and he was feeling very uneasy. Luke had always thought of himself as strong, but he was admittedly afraid, and he didn't feel so strong right now. He didn't want to face those *things* again. He felt safe in Grandpa's basement and wondered how long he could stay down here. Luke lovingly scratched Archie behind his ears to calm him a bit too, and took a few deep breaths to calm himself. He had almost forgotten how terrified they both were just a few short hours ago. Almost. Those unexpected sounds brought it all rushing back, and Luke felt a sense of urgency to bandage himself up so he could finish dressing.

Once Luke was all patched up again, and got his shirt and socks on, he felt a little better, but the noises still rattled him. And even though Luke knew nothing could get in here, he just couldn't shake the sinking feeling that was growing in his gut. He tried to make sense of the sounds. They were very loud and rhythmic, and they just didn't sound the same as the rotting man banging on the door like before. "What if those *were* gunshots boy, what would that mean?" Luke said to Archie. "It would mean someone was in the house, and that someone wasn't one of those things," he continued.

Luke knew there wasn't much he could do about it right now. He couldn't even walk, let alone run, or fight. No, what he needed most now was rest, and some time to heal. Without that, he wouldn't be able to protect Archie or himself, or get to Kate, *if* they could even find her.

In that moment, with that thought, Luke knew exactly what he wanted to do, what he needed to do. Find Kate.

Chapter 17

The Gun Shop

* * *

Jonah slowly drove into the gun shop's parking lot and pulled around to the back and killed the engine. He watched for a few minutes, instructing Sophia to be as quiet as possible. She didn't make a sound as she also looked out of each window with laser focus, then rotating back through them several times more. Jonah rolled down the windows a few inches to listen for another few minutes. Nothing.

"Is it okay?" Sophia said so softly that Jonah almost didn't hear her.

"I think so," Jonah whispered back. "When I was a Ranger, we were in a few situations where it was quiet, just like this, but there were enemy soldiers, hiding, just waiting for the right moment to ambush us. But I don't think these deadheads are intelligent in that way."

Sophia screwed up her face. "Deadheads? That's what you call them?"

"Yeah, I guess I do, that or meatheads," Jonah said.

"That's sort of funny. But yeah, it fits, doesn't it?" Then she got a sad look in her eyes as she looked away from Jonah.

"Yes, but hey listen, let's move and see if we can get in. It's a gun shop, so I'm pretty sure it'll be safe in there if we can get inside. You saw the bars on the windows out front, and we aren't getting through that heavy steel door back here, either. But do you see that fire ladder up there?" Jonah pointed up.

"Yeah," Sophia answered.

"That's our way in, I think." He paused for a moment and cocked his head slightly as he looked at her. "How would you feel if I lifted you up there so you can climb up enough to peek over the top ledge there and see if it looks clear? I'll stay down here and watch our backs. Think you can do that for us?" Jonah placed his hand on her forearm as she rested it on the center console.

"Yeah, okay, sure, I'll do it," she said hesitantly.

"Okay, leave your gun here on the seat, I've got this," Jonah reached into a hidden compartment just behind the console in the back floorboard area and pulled out his Springfield Saint AR-10 pistol. He brought it around front, released the magazine to check it, then clicked it back in place. Then he pulled back on the charging handle, but only partially, to perform a press check. Jonah knew a round was chambered, but this action was automatic for him.

Sophia's eyes grew wider. "Is that from the Army?" She asked excitedly.

"No, but it's close. I'll show you how it works once we get inside. You ready?" Jonah asked.

"Yep, she said," with a hint of excitement in her voice.

"Okay, wait for me to get out and open your door."

"Roger, dodger," she said with a tiny smile

Jonah opened his door as gently as he could, and with a soft push, pressed it shut, standing motionless for a few more moments, listening and scanning for any threats. Still nothing. So he moved around to Sophia's side and opened her door, pressing his index finger to his lips in a shushing gesture. He took Sophia's hand and helped her get down to stand next to him. They were only a few steps from the spot, just under the emergency ladder. Jonah didn't want to linger out in the open any longer than necessary, so he knelt down on the ground to get eye level with Sophia. "You ready?" he asked.

"Ready," she said, with more confidence than he expected.

"Okay, I'll push you up. Just climb high enough to peek over the edge, get a good look, and climb back down. I'll be right here waiting at the bottom of the ladder," Jonah said in a low voice.

"I know," she said.

Jonah could see that she wanted to get this over with, so he didn't waste any time lifting her up to stand on his shoulders. This put the ladder at Sophia's chest level, where she latched on and scurried to the top in a flash.

When she reached the top, Sophia raised her eyes just above the ledge of the roof and scanned from side to side. The roof was empty except for a rusty square metal box with vents on the side, and a small shed with a door in the center. She noticed a big padlock on the door and thought that must lead inside. She climbed back down and Jonah lifted her to the ground.

"There isn't anything up there except a big rusty box and a door with a lock on it," Sophia whispered.

"What kind of lock?" Jonah asked.

"It's the kind that just hangs on the outside," Sophia answered.

"A padlock," Jonah said.

"Yeah, that's it," Sophia confirmed.

"Let's get our gear out of the truck and get up there. We need to get behind cover," Jonah whispered.

Sophia had nothing except the clothes she was wearing, and the Sig Jonah entrusted to her. But Jonah picked that up and tucked it into his waistband, slung his AR-10 over his shoulder, then grabbed a black backpack from the back seat. After he got all his gear situated on his waist and shoulders, he moved to the back of the truck and unlocked a small toolbox under the rear window. Locating what he was looking for there, Jonah grabbed it and then locked everything up.

"Okay, I'm ready, let's move," Jonah said as he looked down at Sophia, who was standing there with her hands on her hips. She had such an expression, Jonah thought. But it was clear what she was thinking as she scanned over Jonah with all the crap he was carrying, and her standing there, empty-handed.

"Um, hey, can you carry this," Jonah said, as he removed the slung AR-10 from his shoulder, made sure the safety selector was in the safe position, and turned her to sling it behind her back. She turned back to face him and smiled.

"Want me to carry anything else?" She asked. "What's that?" she added, as she pointed to the long-handled tool Jonah grabbed from the back of the truck.

"That's our key," Jonah winked. "No, I'll get the rest. Your job is to get up there fast and stand watch while I make my way up."

Jonah pushed Sophia back up to the ladder, turned and did one last quick scan of the area, then hoisted himself up the ladder. The first few rungs had to be hands only, because the first rung was at about 8 feet off the ground. It was nothing for Jonah.

Sophia was up the ladder and over, waiting on the rooftop before Jonah even got his first foot planted on the ladder. Just like a trained soldier, she was scouting all around him as he climbed. Jonah really liked Sophia. She was a smart kid and had amazing instincts for such a young girl; he thought. It didn't take Jonah long to pull himself over a three-foot rooftop wall at the top of the ladder. He stood next to Sophia, placed his hand on her tiny shoulder, "Nice work kiddo," he said, and she beamed up at him for a moment. "You were right, not much up here except that old air conditioning unit and the rooftop door. Let's see if our key works," Jonah said, and began moving toward the door.

Jonah grabbed the old lock and half expected it to break off. It was so aged and rusty, but as he shook it a few times, the sturdy old lock held fast. Jonah positioned the jaws of the large bolt cutters over the lock's shackle and began working the large handles. Sophia watched as Jonah squeezed the handles together, and could see veins popping out in his neck as he strained against the old lock. He removed the tool, repositioned it, and did the same thing again. After the 4th time of repeating this, and using all his strength, the lock's shank snapped. "Man, that was harder than I thought it was gonna be," Jonah huffed, as he wiped sweat from his forehead with the sleeve of his jacket. "Sophia, I want you to stand behind the door, back here, okay?" Jonah walked around the small shed that housed the door. "I don't know what we're going to find on the other side of that door, so when I open it, I want you back here, okay?" Sophia nodded and stood where Jonah had told her, as he moved back around to the door. Jonah removed the padlock from the metal ring it was fitted through and moved the large hasp on its hinge. Jonah positioned himself on the left side of the door, where the doorknob was located, but off to the side. He didn't want to be an easy target for anything that might be on the other side of that door.

Expecting the door to be locked, Jonah was surprised when the doorknob turned freely, and the door clicked open, He pushed it the rest of the way, being careful to stay off to the side, out of the line-of-sight anyone behind the door would have. "Friendly," Jonah declared, as the door moved inward and opened all the way. No reply came, but the stench hit him before the door stopped moving. It was like the others he had smelled, and there was no doubt about what was down there. He gagged, and moved further away from the door to clearer air, and waited and listened.

"What is it?" Sophia whispered.

"I don't know yet, but I think one or more of those things are down there. Stay put while I clear it, okay?"

"Okay," was all she said.

Jonah pulled a large bandanna out of the side pocket of his backpack and tied it around his nose and mouth. It would help some.

"Turn around Cricket," Jonah said, but she just narrowed her eyes at him and didn't move. Sighing, he repeated the request, this time saying, "Turn around Sophia." Now satisfied, she nodded and turned around. Jonah gently lifted the two-point sling over her head. "You'll be safe here. I may need this though," he explained.

She turned to face him and nodded, "Please be careful Jonah," and surprised even herself when she wrapped her arms around his waist in a hug. He patted her back and said, "Always, kiddo, always."

When she pulled away, Jonah gave her a small wink, and turned toward the door. "Stay here until I come back to get you, okay? I won't be long, promise," Jonah said, and pressed a small button to turn on his weapon light and cleared the entrance.

Once inside the doorway, he stood at the top of a stairway landing area and listened carefully. There was no sound, but the smell was awful. Jonah inched his way down the stairs, AR in front of him and raised to his cheek. The powerful light illuminated the full length of the stairway, and nearing the bottom of the stairs, Jonah saw the source of the smell. Two bodies lay just at the bottom landing. One was unquestionably a deadhead, with half its skull missing, splattered all over the wall next to the stairway. The other was a young woman with a bullet hole in her temple. She also had a chunk of flesh ripped from her arm. There was a compact Springfield .45 laying on the ground next to her. It didn't take a detective to figure out what had happened here. The woman clearly didn't want to turn into one of those things after being bitten. It was a shame, Jonah thought. She was a beautiful young woman. "Damn," was all he said.

Jonah spent the next five minutes clearing the rest of the store and found no one else. There were several broken windows, but the bars did their job and kept all the would-be intruders out. Jonah made his way back to the stairs and figured that these two most likely knew each other. Maybe they worked here, though he didn't recognize either of them.

Sprinting back up the stairs, he was relieved to be back outside in the fresh air. "Sophia," he called out as he moved to where she sat waiting for him, back against the wall.

"Hey!" she said, relieved. "Everything okay?"

"Yeah, well, sort of," Jonah replied. "I have good news and bad news. Which do you want to hear first?"

"I really need some good news, so good news, please?"

"We have a safe place to stay for a little while, and it would be next to impossible for any of those things to get in here."

"Then what's the bad news?" she asked, pitch rising as she said each word.

"There's one of those things down there now. It's dead, but it stunk up the place. I need to get it out of there before we can go down there." Jonah purposely left out the part about the young woman.

"Can I help you?" she offered bravely.

"No, trust me, you really don't want to go down there. Let me go find something to wrap it up with, and I'll drag it up here. Can you wait here while I do that?" he asked.

"Okay, but please hurry."

"Roger, dodger," he said, and hurried back down the stairs.

Sophia sat there thinking about her mom, trying not to cry, and trying to make sense of all that she had seen. She had heard about zombies before and had even read a few books about them. Her favorite was *The Last Kids on Earth* series. But she never thought they could be real. It was like the fairytales her mom read to her when she was really little. They were impossible to be real, right? But the monsters here were real, and they killed her mother. She was glad she met Jonah. He seemed nice, and she felt safe with him. But she really missed her mom. She didn't have anyone else, no brothers, no sisters, no dad. She had never met her dad. Her mom talked about him all the time though and even had pictures of him on her dresser and over the fireplace. He died when she was a baby. All her mom would say was that he was a hero, and that he flew planes for the Navy, off of those big aircraft carriers. She loved him, though, even though she never met him. Well, she guessed she met him when she was a baby, but she didn't remember any of that. She wished she could remember.

Lost in her thoughts, Jonah startled her when he suddenly appeared, gasping for air, and sweating again, despite the cold.

"You okay?" he asked.

"Yea, are you?" she mocked back.

"Very funny. Yeah. I got that thing out of there and dragged him over to the far edge of the roof. It's still really stinky down there, but I don't think it will take too long to air out. Some windows down there are busted out."

"You said it was safe there though," she interrupted.

"It is. They all have bars over them, and nothing can get past those. Trust me," he reassured her. "I also found a can of Lysol spray in the bathroom and sprayed it all around until it was empty. It didn't help much, but anything is better than nothing. Want to wait a while and give it some time, or do you want to head down and see if we can figure out our next move?" Thunder cracked overhead, and that seemed to make up her mind for her.

"Let's go inside. I don't want to get rained on. It's cold."

"Your wish is my command," he said, and extended his hand to help her up.

Funny, she was just thinking about fairytales...

Chapter 18

Safe, For Now

***

Crack! Boom!

Loud thunder gave way to large drops of rain. The torrent came out of nowhere as Jonah and Sophia made a quick dash around to the door. When Sophia rounded the corner, she noticed two wrapped bundles against the ledge of the roof, near where they had climbed over. She could tell the two heaps were both bodies. *Why did he only tell me there was one,* she wondered, as she lingered just a moment longer to study them? She gave Jonah a sideways glance. Jonah shrugged stupidly as he was being pelted by enormous raindrops. Sophia, already under the cover of the entryway, narrowed her eyes at him, forcing him to stand there with that stupid look on his face for a few seconds longer. Then she turned and disappeared through the door.

As he came through the metal door, he pulled it closed hard behind him, feeling the water squish inside his boots. *Crap,* he thought, *those are gonna take forever to dry.* Jonah picked up a rather thick metal bar laying on the floor, just inside the door, and dropped it into place through its holders on each side of the doorjamb. He wondered why it wasn't on in the first place, but thankful that it wasn't, otherwise, they never would have gotten inside. A scenario played out in his mind of the young woman he'd found at the bottom of the stairs, and how she must have tried to escape through the rooftop door from that deadhead, but couldn't because it was padlocked from the outside. He could imagine the terror she must have felt.

"Man, it's really coming down!" Jonah said, but Sophia was already at the bottom of the stairs, looking around the shop. She didn't even hear him.

Jonah was suddenly feeling very self-conscious. How could that 13-year-old little girl have such an effect on him? He wondered. Realizing he was soaked, and she wasn't, made him shake his head. Running his fingers through his hair a few times to help him shed off some of the water, he called down to her, "Stay away from the windows. There's a lot of broken glass, okay?"

"Okay," was all she said.

Jonah made his way down the stairs and joined her. She was looking through the glass of one of the large handgun displays.

"I like that one," she said, pointing at a large shiny revolver. "What is it?"

"That's a Smith and Wesson .500 Magnum. It's a beast. I fired one once, and it kicks like a mule. Hey, it's getting cold in here, and I'm hungry, and tired," Jonah said. Then he looked down at his soaked clothes and added, "And now I'm all wet, too." Sophia just looked at him. It wasn't hard to see the wheels turning behind those green eyes of hers. But she remained silent as she moved her gaze to the back room.

"What's back there?" She asked.

"It's a small office area. I saw a fridge back there," Jonah added, in a playful voice, and waited for a reaction, knowing she must be just as hungry as he was. But he didn't get one. *She's one tough little girl*, he thought. She walked over to a large set of shelves that contained countless small boxes of varying shapes and colors; bullets, she suspected.

"Can these help us?" Sophia asked.

"Yep, and there's a lot of other stuff in here that can help us too, but right now, food and rest are what we need the most. C'mon, let's go see what we can find back there," Jonah said, nodding in the direction of the back room.

Jonah raised his AR and pressed the button to activate its light again. It was light outside, but the stormy weather made it feel more dusk-like, and it was dark in the back room area. Sophia moved close to Jonah and surprised him when she pressed her small hand against his back. Together, they passed by the registers and went through an open doorway that led to a storage area, and then into a small office. The space was well organized and nothing seemed to be out of place, and that was a good sign for Jonah. Several floor-to-ceiling shelves lined two walls and held a large assortment of firearms still in their manufacturer boxes. Jonah noticed a large, well-worn cardboard box on the bottom shelf closest to the office area, and he shone his light inside and saw some blankets and pillows neatly stacked inside it.

"Boy, we can sure use those," Jonah said, relieved to discover them. The last thing he wanted was for the two of them to have to sleep on the cold, hard floor.

Once they moved past the shelves, there was an old, well-kept desk tucked in a corner, a matching filing cabinet next to it, and a large safe next to that. In the middle of the open area stood a workbench with a couple of tall stools around it. A full-sized refrigerator stood against the wall next to the door to a small bathroom. The entire area was less than 20-feet square but it was laid out very efficiently. Jonah was quite taken by how clean and tidy everything was. There didn't seem to be a single thing out of place. It reminded him of the old black-and-white TV shows he liked so much. Then he thought of The Twilight Zone, one of his favorites, and in that moment felt that's exactly where *they* were.

Jonah decided it would be safe to flip on the lights, but when he found the light switch on the wall, it was already on. He flipped it the other way. Nothing.

"Oh great," he huffed.

"What?" Sophia asked.

"No power. Looks like we're in the dark, kiddo."

He went to the fridge and opened it. No light there either. But it was still cold inside, so he closed it to keep it that way for now.

"Looks like we have some food, though," Jonah said. "Let's get cleaned up, have something to eat, and then try to get some rest. That sound okay?"

"I need to pee," Sophia announced.

Jonah waved the light in the direction of the small bathroom, which he cleared earlier, and smiled at her. "In there," he said.

"It's dark in there!"

"Hang on, I've got something for you."

Jonah swung his backpack to the floor, unzipped a pocket on the side, and pulled out a small flashlight for Sophia.

"Here ya go," he said, and handed it to her. "Keep it after you're done in there."

"Thanks," she said as she snatched it out of his hand and disappeared into the bathroom.

Jonah dug through his pack and pulled out a small battery-powered lantern and placed it on the workbench and switched it on, then turned off his weapon light. He also pulled out a dry t-shirt, some socks, and a lightweight pair of cargo pants. Jonah also pocketed the only other light he carried in his pack, which was a small penlight with a red lens. He didn't carry an extra pair of boots or shoes; those would have been too bulky for his go-bag, so he'd just have to hope his would dry quickly. After zipping up his pack, he went over to the fridge and pulled out a few things and placed them on the workbench. It was a good haul, and there was still more in there.

Jonah heard the toilet flushing and expected Sophia to appear at any moment, so he reached down and picked up the bundle of dry clothes. Just as he straightened, the bathroom door flung open and out sprang Sophia. She hopped up on one stool and studied the spread.

"I'll be right back, dig in," Jonah said, and left his small companion to go into the bathroom to change. Closing the door, he turned on his penlight and sat it on the counter. It made little light, but it was enough. He'd used something similar plenty of times when deployed. The red light had a much lower light profile than a white light, and it helped preserve a soldier's night vision. Jonah went to the sink first and scrubbed the crud off his face and hands. After that, he changed his clothes, and then he filled his boots with wads of toilet paper and hung them on a hook that was on the bathroom door, figuring he'd remove the toilet paper before going to sleep. He remembered showing Luke that trick on a hunting trip a few years ago when Luke slipped into an icy stream and didn't have a spare pair of boots with him. "Luke!" Jonah slapped his forehead and bounced to his jacket and reached into an inside pocket and pulled out his phone. Jonah felt guilty for not thinking of his old friend sooner, but he had been running for his life for the past several hours. Tapping the phone icon, Jonah pressed recents and then Luke. He waited for Luke to answer, but it immediately went to voicemail. "Luke, hey Bro, I hope you're okay. Crazy what's happening, right? Listen, I'm okay and I'm coming to you as soon as I can. Maybe a day or so. I don't know exactly. Man, I really hope you're okay. Please be safe. Wait for me there if you can, okay? I hope you're alright, Bro. Call me, please." Jonah was worried. Luke's phone must be dead. He tried again with no luck.

Jonah left the small bathroom and brought his wet clothes with him. He draped them over various places around the room so they could dry.

He had only been gone five minutes tops, but when he made it back to the workbench, Sophia had already prepared sandwiches and chips for both of them and placed them on napkins. She'd even found a couple of plastic cups and filled them with the orange juice he had set out.

Jonah, impressed that she'd prepared everything so fast, said, "Thanks! This looks great Sophia. Mind if I say a little prayer before we eat?" She didn't say a word, but closed her eyes and interlaced her fingers together under her chin.

Jonah prayed, "Heavenly Father, thank you Lord for providing for us and for keeping us safe. We need you now more than ever. Please continue to watch over us and protect us. Amen."

"And please tell my Mom that I love her and that I'm sorry. Amen," Sophia added.

Jonah went all soft at hearing that, and held his hands just a little longer so he wouldn't have to speak, feeling all choked up.

As they ate their ham sandwiches and Lay's potato chips, they said little, except small talk, like, pass a napkin, or, are there more chips, and the like. There were also two apples on the workbench and those disappeared too after the sandwiches and chips were gone.

"Why did you lie to me?"

Sophia didn't say a lot, but when she did, she didn't beat around the bush. Jonah liked that about her. But he didn't like this question.

"What do you mean?" Jonah knew, but hoped it was something else.

"You said there was only one, but there were two bodies up there. Why did you lie?"

"I didn't lie Cricket."

"You did, and stop calling me that!"

"I'm sorry, Sophia. I didn't lie. I just didn't want to tell you about the other one I found, because I didn't want it to upset you."

"I had to shoot my own mom because she turned into one of those things. You don't have to spare my feelings. Tell me the truth!"

The way she said it; so serious, so grown up, Jonah couldn't believe he was talking to a 13-year-old. Everything about this girl was far beyond her years, except her small stature.

"I'm sorry. I told you before I'd make some mistakes. But I didn't lie exactly. There was *only* one deadhead. The second one was a young woman, not one of those things."

"Then how did she..." Sophia trailed off, thinking about it before finishing. "She killed herself, didn't she?"

"That's what it looked like to me, Sophia. It had bitten her on her arm and I think she didn't want to end up like the thing she had just killed."

"I don't want to end up like that either, Jonah. Please don't lie to me again. Trying to protect me from the truth won't help me survive."

There was some truth in what she said, Jonah thought.

"Okay. I Promise kiddo."

She walked over to him and punched him in the arm.

Jonah mocked pain, then asked, "Sophia, can I ask you something?"

"You just—"

"I know, I just did," Jonah interrupted, then smiled. "Where's your dad?"

"He's dead too."

"I'm sorry Sophia."

"It's okay. I mean, I never really knew him. I was just a baby when he died. But I know my mom really loved him, and that makes me love him, too."

"Do you know what happened?"

"Yeah, my mom always told me the truth about everything," she said, and looked right into Jonah's eyes for a few long seconds, as if to remind him he *had* lied to her. "He was a Navy pilot and his plane crashed. Mom had pictures of him all over our house. I think he was kind of handsome, like you," she added, but then looked away quickly in embarrassment, cheeks turning red, not meaning to let that slip out.

Jonah's face flushed a little too, and he tried not to let his own embarrassment show. "I lost some good friends when I was in the Army, too. It sucks, I know. Do you know what type of aircraft your father flew?"

"Mom said he flew fighter jets from aircraft carriers. She had a bunch of pictures of him in his uniform on the ships and in his plane."

"Sophia, those Naval pilots are some serious bad asses. Um, I mean, really great soldiers."

Sophia giggled and threw her hand over her mouth. It was the first time Jonah saw her act like a 13-year-old. He was glad he got to see that. Even if it did take him accidentally cursing to get her to show it.

"Seriously though, I got to meet some of them when I was in Afghanistan for some joint missions we did together. They were really great guys, and talk about funny. They cracked up more than us Rangers did."

"Rangers?" Sophia asked.

"Yeah, I was an Army Ranger. We were a kind of special combat unit in the Army and did things that other soldiers weren't trained for. We were a close group, like brothers. Anyway, you should be really proud of your dad. There aren't many men in the world who can do what he did. We were all pretty much in awe of those Navy fighter pilots. Folks said that about us Rangers too, but I can tell you as a Ranger myself, those Navy flyers were in a whole different league."

Jonah didn't expect what happened next. Sophia wrapped her arms around him in a tight hug around his waist. Her head barely reached his chest, and that's where she hid her face. He didn't know quite what to do, so he just stood there awkwardly for a moment, frozen. But then he put one arm around her shoulders and stood there until she moved away.

"Thanks Jonah," was all she said.

"Um, are you okay?"

"Yeah, I'm good," she said, as she wiped her eyes quickly.

"Hey, I found something over near the desk you can use to get some sleep if you're tired."

She walked over to the desk so he wouldn't see her red cheeks and found what she thought he was talking about.

"A fold up chair?" She puzzled.

"No, it's a cot. Think of it like a portable bed. Pull it out of the corner and set it up. I'll go grab some blankets and pillows for you from that big box."

Thankful for the unexpected comforts, Jonah grabbed all the blankets and pillows from the box and carried them back into the small office. Sophia was already laying on the cot, testing it this way, and that.

"I've never seen one of these before," she said, as she sat up on her elbows.

"Yeah, they sure beat sleeping on the hard floor."

"What about you? Where will you sleep?"

"Don't worry about me. I'll be fine. Hey, I saw a toothbrush and toothpaste in the bathroom. I have an unused one in my pack. You can have it. I'll use the one in the bathroom."

Jonah walked over to his pack and pulled out some floss and the toothbrush. Handing them to Sophia, he said, "You go first. I'll straighten up a bit in here."

"Thank you."

"Sure," Jonah said.

Before long, Sophia sandwiched herself between two warm blankets on top of the cot behind the desk and had a soft pillow under her head. Jonah spread his pallet out near the open door along the wall. Though he expected nothing to get into their small fortress, anything coming through the door wouldn't likely see him right away, tucked up against the wall the way he was. Jonah turned off the small lantern and climbed between his two blankets. He placed his AR on top of his blanket against the wall beside him and he held his Sig in his hand under the blanket as he closed his eyes. Jonah was almost asleep when he heard Sophia ask, "What are we going to do, Jonah?"

"I've thought a lot about that. My best friend has a big house a few miles from here. We grew up together. He's really the only family I have." Jonah felt a sudden pang of sadness for Sophia at that moment. "Except you," he added.

Sophia couldn't believe he said that. It affected her in a way she didn't understand, but she was so glad he did. Under her blankets, she clenched her hands together, squeezed her eyes shut, and whispered, "Thank you, God."

"What's his name?"

"Luke. You'll like him. He's a great guy, and he has a massive dog that you'll love. I have to go check on him, Sophia, to make sure he's okay. Then I think all of us should get away from here and find a safe place to stay, to wait this out. Some place away from people, if we can."

She liked the sound of that. Sophia didn't understand any of this, but she knew it was dangerous around all these people, things, whatever they were.

"For now, let's get some sleep," Jonah said. "We need it. And without rest, we won't think clearly. If we're going to survive, we have to use our brains. So, when we wake up, we'll have some breakfast and then training begins. I promised I'd protect you, and that includes teaching you how to protect yourself. Get some sleep. Night, Cricket."

She didn't correct him that time.

"Night, Jonah."

Sophia didn't say anything else, but once more, under her warm blankets, she squeezed her hands and eyes tight and whispered, "Thank you."

Chapter 19

Gramps

* * *

Luke sat down on the lower bunk that he'd picked out for himself. He placed one of the oil lamps he'd found on the small table next to the bunk and lit it, then he flicked off his flashlight. He set the oil lamp's wick to a comfortable light level and then leaned back on the bunk's headboard, which was really just the wall. As Luke lay there thinking about what to do next, he looked at Archie laying on the floor next to him, and felt so thankful to have his furry friend here with him. He was sure he wouldn't even be alive if it weren't for Archie. His eyes drifted upward as he lay there, and he suddenly opened them wider. There, just under the bunk above him, zip-tied to the metal criss-cross frame supporting the mattress above him, was a red notebook in a large ziplock baggie. Luke suddenly felt as if he had found the lost treasure of Atlantis and he sat up quickly and reached for it with eager fingers to pull it loose. When he got it down, he felt a pang of sadness in his heart as he saw his grandpa's neatly printed handwriting on the cover in small block letters. It simply said: *For Emma and Luke: Emergency Instructions.* Luke slid it out of the now torn bag and opened the notebook cover, and right there on the very first page was a letter written in the very same handwriting that Luke knew so well. Gramps had the most amazing handwriting and Luke had always thought it looked like a machine made it because it was so neat and perfect. It was all print, and every letter was exactly the same height and width. Luke was always envious of his grandfather's handwriting because his own left-handed chicken scratch was so messy. The letter said:

* * *

My sweet Emma, and my dear boy Luke, if you're reading this, then you're probably in trouble. If you're not in trouble, then put this notebook back where you found it (Luke). If you are in trouble, then keep reading. The most important thing you can do right now is to lock the door at the top of the stairs with the large iron bar. STOP WHAT YOU'RE DOING AND GO LOCK THAT DOOR. Nothing smaller than a bulldozer will be able to get through it.

Now that you've locked the door, take a few deep breaths and try to remain calm. You are safe here. I know you're probably afraid right now. That's okay, I've been afraid plenty in my life. But the most important thing to remember is that you can't let your fear cause you to make poor decisions. That will get you killed, and the whole point of me making this place was to keep you alive. So breathe, and let me help you through the first few things you need to do. You are both stronger than you know and you will be okay, so read on.

Luke wiped a single tear from his cheek. He really missed his Gramps, and his quiet yet strong demeanor. He was always looking out for them, and even though he was gone now, he was still looking out for them. Luke hadn't realized how alone and afraid he was until just this moment and reading grandpa's letter really moved Luke. "This is just like you, Gramps. I love you. Thanks for everything," Luke said softly to his grandpa. He read on.

There are enough supplies stored down here to last you for a long time, at least a year. This notebook will help you understand how things work down here and what you ought to do. It's organized into sections, and each section is important, so please read them all. But you don't have to do that just now. I wrote the most important things in this short letter. Do them first, and you can come back to the details in each section later, after you've rested up some.

1. If you need first aid, there is a large medical box marked with a big Red Cross in the bathroom. It's got everything from pain meds, to antibiotics, to sutures and bandaids. There's also a book in there to explain certain medical procedures that you may have to do for yourself, like giving yourself or someone else stitches.

2. If you need something to protect yourself, there is a shotgun and ammo on the shelf next to the stairs. You both know how to use it. Just point it and shoot, and you'll hit anything in front of you. There are more firearms and self-defense items in the gun safe inside this room. The combination is: 33662# If the battery is dead, there's a key taped inside the back cover of this notebook.

3. There is running water in the bathroom that is fed by a well I had dug. The water is clean and good. Solar panels power the well pump on the roof, so you should have running water. If that doesn't work, there is a manual pump handle inside the locker next to the shower. It's right next to the large pressurized water tank. It's got a big red handle on it, so you can't miss it. Pump the handle 20 times to create enough pressure to run the water. Emma, it's not that hard to pump, so don't worry, I got the easiest one I could find.

4. I connected the solar panels to a bunch of big batteries I have stored inside the basement. So if you don't have power down here, you'll need to switch over to the solar power. To do that, locate the small breaker box on the wall inside the "dirt room". You'll know it when you see it. Open the door on that box and flip off the city power breaker. I painted it bright yellow, so you can't miss it. Then slide down the big metal plate painted red. Once you've done that, you can flip on the breaker painted bright green. This will turn on power to everything down here.

Luke stopped reading, gently laid the red notebook face down on the bed, and carefully got to his feet. Archie immediately stood up too, because he didn't want to miss out on any adventure Luke might be off to. Luke grabbed his flashlight and walked to the dirt room as quickly as his aching ankle would allow him. He found the breaker box exactly how Gramps had described it and switched it over to solar power. When he did, the room lit up, and he could also see light outside the door too. "Gramps, you sly old fox," Luke said. "Big Bear, we've been living like animals down here in the dark. Uh, no offense," Luke smiled down at his companion and ruffled the top of his head. Archie started jumping around Luke's feet. Boy, it was really starting to smell in this room and Luke knew he had to deal with that problem pretty soon. "Hey boy, let's go see what we can see now," Luke said as he rubbed the side of Archie's face.

Luke made his way back to the bunk room and was happy to see a couple of overhead LED lights illuminated. It really helped a lot and instantly made him feel better. Archie even had more spring in his step now that the lights were finally on. It somehow didn't seem so hopeless. Luke knew they were still in big trouble, but he felt just a little more hopeful now. He felt like Gramps was right there with them.

Luke settled back down on the bunk and flicked on the small light above his head that was mounted on the bunk frame. The light was so much better now. Luke picked up the red notebook and began reading where he'd left off.

5. I've stored plenty of food down here, and there's a gas stove on the back wall of the main room. It works, and there are matches in a small ceramic box sitting on the shelf next to the stove. Use those to light a burner if the igniter doesn't work. It's an old stove, and it's finicky. I meant to fix that igniter, but never got around to it. There are cases of food on the shelf next to the stove, too. There's plenty more stored in several places I'll tell you about later, if you haven't found it already. But I figured you'd be hungry and wouldn't want to hunt too hard to find something to eat, so it's there right next to the stove. Eat up, you need your strength. Don't ever forget that. Your brain can't function properly without food and we have plenty down here to eat. And your brains are going to be working overtime to get through whatever is happening in the world right now.

Luke shook his head and laughed at himself. The matches were right there all the time, and he didn't even bother to look. His stomach growled and Archie looked up at him. It was definitely time to eat. "Hang on, boy, we'll eat a big meal in a few minutes. I know you must be hungry, too. Just let me read a bit more of grandpa's letter first, okay?"

Luke read on.

6. If there was a nuclear event, you're still going to be pretty safe down here. The basement and its rooms aren't airtight, but pretty darn close. I've also got quite a good air filtration system down here that won't require much on your part. Just keep the one door closed and locked, and don't open it before you read the section of this book labeled "Nuclear Event". It's important, so don't skip it if that's what happened. Don't fool with it if that's not what happened. You'll have more important things to do.

7. There's hot water for the shower and sink. It's on gas too, and the propane tank should be full. Only the water heater and the stove use gas down here. I never got around to putting in a clothes dryer, but there is a washing machine in the small room next to the bathroom. You'll have to hang your clothes to dry if you ever get around to washing them. Take a shower and get cleaned up. It'll make you feel better. There are plenty of clean clothes for both of you down here. Just look around and you'll find them.

8. You may need to charge up your phone or other devices. In the brown metal cabinet in the dirt room there's a bunch of spare batteries, a box of phone charging cables and such, and even a portable charging station (in case you can't get the power on in here). I've added a few different kinds of mobile phone chargers. I also put a multi-band radio in the closet on a small shelf in this bunk room. You can use that to get some news if you don't have anything else.

There's a lot more to tell you, but it can wait. Treat your wounds if you have any, and get something to eat. Then rest yourselves. You're going to need it. Come back to this book in a day or two if things calm down a bit.

* * *

Luke thought for a moment about his phone and where it could be. He really wished that he had it now so he could try to reach Kate and Jonah. Not knowing what was happening out there, or if they were okay or not, was the hardest part of all. Besides Archie, they were all the family he had in the world. He was sure he had dropped it somewhere during his and Archie's struggles to get to the basement, but he had no idea where. It could be in a thousand different places in the house, and he couldn't get to any of them right now. It was probably on the floor somewhere under a couch or a table, with as many times as he had fallen or had been knocked to the floor. The last thing he remembered was that it was dead, but he couldn't remember the last time he'd seen it. He tried to think hard on that, but he just couldn't remember. He'd come back to that thought later. Luke continued reading.

* * *

Well, that's about it for now. I love you both more than anything in the whole world. You are both the sunshine of my life, and I'm real sorry that I'm not there to help you now, but I've made a safe place for you here. Oh, that reminds me, the last part of this notebook is about the cabin. You're going to want to read that part if you need to get out of Dodge. You see, this world has been in the crapper for a lot of years. Between the commies in Russia, North Korea, and China, and the terrorists in the Middle East, our way of life here in the good old USA has been in danger for a long time. For the past ten years or so, I've felt it in my bones that something bad is coming. Not sure what it will be, but we've been living under the pretense of safety and security for far too long for it to hold. There are too many evil people in this world that want to take what we have, and even our government has become a corrupt mess. Money is worthless. They've killed off God, and they continue to take our freedom away piece by piece, slowly, so we don't see it happening, but they are doing it just the same. That's why I built this bunker for you, and why there's another place for you to go to when it's time to leave here. There's lots in this notebook to help you and I've tried to think of everything, but I'm sure I've missed something along the way. I'm sorry if I did. So here's what you're going to do: You're going to remember that God loves us, and that Jesus died for us so that we can live with him forever with love and peace like you can't imagine. But you might have to go through hell first, Boy. Heck, even the Bible says so, but you remember, He's coming. So remember to keep saying your prayers and lean on the Lord. He'll take care of you.

Love, Gramps.

Tears were flowing freely down Luke's face now and he didn't even bother to wipe them away. He just stared at his grandpa's notebook and what he had written there, and he just let it all out. Archie had jumped up on the small bunk by this point, and they were both there on that small bed, in this small room, with their small LED light, and just sat there close to each other. Emotions heavy, Luke hugged Archie and let the tears fall on the thick fur around his neck. He didn't know how long he sat there like that with Archie, but eventually, they both just drifted off to sleep.

Chapter 20

The Radio

* * *

Bark! Bark!

Luke's eyes snapped open to see Archie standing next to the bunk, looking right at him. Luke knew that look, so he gingerly got up and led Archie to the dirt room to do his business.

"Well, Big Bear, let's get this over with, shall we?" Luke said, with resolve. Archie cocked his head sideways and looked at Luke with his tongue hanging out.

Luke grabbed a small shovel that he felt he could handle without too much trouble and got to work. Fifteen minutes later, and Luke had managed to bury all of Archie's doings so far, from the time they'd spent down in grandpa's basement.

"Sure am glad that's over with. Let's eat, boy," Luke said with genuine enthusiasm. No, it wasn't the most appetizing chore, but Luke was so hungry he didn't think twice about the task he'd just completed, and he knew Archie didn't care either.

Bark! Bark! Archie replied, and started hopping around Luke's feet like a playful 90-pound puppy.

145

One of Archie's funny traits was his bunny hop. Ever since he was a puppy, whenever he got excited, he would hop straight up into the air with all four feet off the ground. At first, Luke thought it was because Archie didn't quite know how to stand on his hind legs yet, to put his front paws on Luke, but as it turned out, he still did the same thing to this day. He looked like a giant bunny when he did that and it always made Luke smile, and usually drew a goofy smile from Archie as well.

"Are you my big bunny, Archie?" Luke ruffled the top of Archie's head. Archie Jumped up again.

They hurried on their way to the gas stove, and Luke made short work of opening two cans of Chunky Sirloin Burger soup for Archie, emptying them into a large bowl he'd found, and then heating up two cans of Chef Boyardee Beef Ravioli in tomato and meat sauce for himself. Luke remembered eating tons of that stuff when he was a kid, but he hadn't had any in years. Gramps sure remembered how much he loved it though, and had stocked several cases of it, along with Beefaroni in tomato and meat sauce, and Campbells Spaghet-tiOs with Meatballs.

Archie finished his meal quickly, but Luke wasn't far behind.

Luke let out a loud burp, "Ahh, that was good!" Archie looked up at him expectantly.

Luke reached down and placed his nearly empty pot on the floor for Archie to finish off. Luke had avoided using dishes that he didn't absolutely need, to keep the number of things to wash to a minimum. Besides, eating straight out of the pot made him feel a bit like a cowboy out on the trail.

Luke reached for the neat row of empty cans he'd lined up on the left side of the stovetop, and one by one he held them down for Archie to lick clean, which was a treat for Archie. After he spent a minute or two tidying up and washing Archie's bowl, and his own pot and spoon, Luke made his way back to the bunk room. It was time to see if he could get grandpa's radio working.

Luke plopped down on the bunk and rubbed his sore ankle for a moment. He moved it in small circles, testing its range of motion. It was definitely feeling better, but he wouldn't be going on any hiking trips anytime soon. Archie was lying on the floor next to Luke and seemed to be settling in for a nice nap. The radio was sitting on the small table next to the bunk. Luke started to reach for it but then stopped himself. Was he ready to learn what had turned his world upside down, yet? What had almost killed him and his loyal companion? It felt as if a million explanations were flooding his brain all at once, but none of them made any sense. Luke knew what he saw, and he knew what it looked like. But he wouldn't allow himself to believe it.

Taking a deep breath, he reached for the radio and picked it up. It was time; he decided. Luke needed to know what was really happening out there. He tried to turn it on, but nothing happened. After pressing a few different buttons, he decided that the internal battery was dead. He thought for a moment about using the hand crank on the side but decided that would be too much work right now, and plugged it into the power outlet next to the table instead. Luke raised the small antenna and powered it on. Lights came on and he turned up the volume. There was a muffled static sound coming from the speaker now. Okay, step one complete; the radio seemed to work. Now it was time to see if he could pickup any stations. He wasn't familiar with the shortwave band, so he started with the FM band.

At first, Luke moved the dial on the side of the radio quickly, hopeful that something would come in right away. It didn't. Then he started over, this time moving more slowly. He continued to only pick up a bit of static across the frequencies. Once or twice he thought he'd heard a voice, but it was gone as fast as it came. After performing this slow move back and forth on the FM band three times, he gave up and switched it to the AM band. Luke moved as slowly as he could along the AM dial, but once again, only received various levels of static on all the frequencies for his efforts. He was nearing the end of the band when, through a bit of static, he heard the familiar call letters: KRIB. His Gramps listened to the Oldies on this station all the time and Luke had a lot of memories hanging out with his grandpa while those old songs played in the background. He felt a sudden burst of joy at the sound he was receiving, but then it faded to static.

"No, no," Luke sighed in frustration.

He tried again, and again, moving the antenna this way and that, but nothing close to a human voice came in. Luke switched off the radio, somewhat annoyed. Laying there, he thought for a moment. There had to be a way to improve reception from down here. As he thought about it more, he remembered all the copper pipes he'd helped his Gramps haul down here when he was a kid. Copper was a great conductor, he knew, and wondered if they could somehow help him gain better reception. Luke snapped his fingers. "The bathroom!"

With a plan, and a bit of enthusiasm, Luke made his way to the bathroom, while Archie seemed content to just lay there and continue enjoying his nap.

When Luke made it into the bathroom, he looked up and saw the row of copper pipes running across the ceiling. Glad that it was low enough to reach without needing a chair or a ladder, Luke studied the situation for a moment. It would be awkward to just stand there holding the antenna against the pipe, and then he'd still have to operate the radio while holding it above his head. No, that wouldn't be sustainable for any length of time. Remembering a shelf in the dirt room that held several tools and construction materials, Luke left the bathroom and returned in short order with a small roll of electrical wire and a pair of wire cutters. Within five minutes, Luke was sitting comfortably on the toilet seat cover with the radio in his lap. The antenna was extended to full height and a coil of wire was spiraled around the full length of the antenna. The other end of the wire was stretched to one of the copper pipes in the ceiling and coiled a dozen times around that as well. Mentally crossing his fingers, Luke powered on the radio again. Deciding to stick with the AM band, he tuned the radio to 1490 KRIB. He was excited when a clear signal came through the small speaker. Music was not playing, though.

It was some sort of recorded message of the station's call sign, followed by that annoying squelching alarm of the Emergency Broadcasting System. A shaky male voice then began, what could only be described as a fictitious radio drama? It made Luke think of that old 1930s Orson Welles radio broadcast, "War of the Worlds".

Luke tried to make himself comfortable on the hard toilet seat lid as he listened intently to the message. A message that would change his world forever.

Chapter 21

The Message

* * *

From an undisclosed location somewhere on the eastern seaboard of the United States of America, the Secretary of Defense, Andrew T. McPherson, 'Mack' to his friends, stood next to the desk where the microphone was waiting for him to deliver a speech. It was a speech that he was simply not prepared to give. Not that he couldn't say the words. Mack just couldn't believe *he* would be the one saying them. His heart was heavy, and the message was one that, just three days ago, would have been unthinkable. Unbelievable even.

"What the hell am I doing here?" he huffed to himself. "I'm just an old soldier. I don't belong here," he trailed off.

His temporary assistant, Ms. Angelina Hargrave, a lovely and very fit woman of 38, with raven black hair pulled back into a tight ponytail, placed her hand on his back and gently nudged him in the chair's direction. "It's time, Mr. President," she said softly. "We go live in 90 seconds. Please have a seat and try to take a few deep breaths. I'll be right here with you. Can I get you some water, sir?" she asked, in a confident, yet softly feminine voice.

"No, thank you Ms. Hargrave, I'll be fine," Mack replied in his gruff midwestern voice.

Mack looked like a giant next to the petite Ms. Hargrave, and was built like a tank. With his stout 6'4" frame, and hard as iron physique, he was the perfect representation of a commanding Army General. Though he was 68 years old, he could take most men half his age. He was an imposing man and commanded with complete authority. Today, however, Mack was somber and thoughtful.

"Please sir, call me Angie. I think we've been through enough together for you to call me by my first name." She gave him a soft pat on the shoulder as he sat down in the chair.

That was true. They had been, and they almost didn't make it. Half of their Secret Service detail had been tackled to the ground and eaten alive as they were ushered into the bunker.

"Thank you, Angie," he said with an ever so slight, but genuine smile.

"Mr. President, just watch the teleprompter. Take your time. We'll go at your pace. You're on in 3, 2, 1," she trailed off.

* * *

"My fellow Americans, my Countrymen and Women," he began softly. "My name is General Andrew McPherson. Some of you may recognize my name, others may not. I'm the Secretary of Defense of the United States of America. Well, at least I used to be."

His voice cracked and trembled a bit. "We've lost a lot of good people, and it seems I've been promoted. It is with tremendous sorrow that I must inform you that I have assumed the role of President of the United States of America."

Mack had to take a few moments to regain his composure.

General McPherson was *not* reading from the teleprompter, and

Angie started to move to him, but Senator Jackson gently grabbed her arm. "It's fine, Angie, let him speak. He's doing just fine. If we need anything right now, it's truth and sincerity."

"I know," she said matter-of-factly. "I'm just bringing him a glass of water."

Jackson let her go, and as she turned to walk away, he could see the glistening of tears on her cheek.

Angie brought the General a cool glass of water. He smiled at her, "Thank you," he said softly, and took a sip.

Mack continued speaking into the microphone. "If you can hear my voice, I'm so very thankful for that. You're one of the lucky ones, and perhaps it means you're safe. At least I hope it does. I'm sure that all of you know by now that something has gone terribly wrong. Here's what we know: Approximately three days ago, in an unprecedented attack, a deadly super virus was released in multiple regions within our Nation's borders, by an unknown enemy. At least, we believe it's a virus. Our limited intelligence indicates that it can be little else. We do not know of any event in the history of mankind that has propagated so quickly, or of any that has been so catastrophically deadly. The virus appears to have a 100% transmission and mortality rate. The most unique and horrific behavior is that the carriers actively, and aggressively, pursue victims to infect."

Mack knew that the word, *infect,* was an understatement, but it didn't feel appropriate to say *eat people.*

"Our scientists do not even have a classification for an event or behavior such as this. It's as close to an extinction-level event that mankind has ever seen. Well, perhaps besides the great flood described in the Holy Bible in the book of Genesis."

The General took a deep breath. "You've seen what it does to people... we all have. I'm not telling you this to frighten you. I'm telling you this to help keep you safe. I'm telling you this to help keep you alive. I'm telling you this, so that you understand you must do all you can to avoid contact with those who are infected. That is, if you can do so without putting others in harm's way. This virus mutates its host, changes them physiologically in a way that makes them nearly unrecognizable."

General McPherson paused for a few long moments, and then continued, "There is just no way to sugarcoat this, and I'm not one to mince words. Never have been. Once this occurs, the host, or carrier, seems to have a singular purpose, and that is to attack others indiscriminately. We do not believe there can be a cure for this virus once infected. The hosts appear to change so rapidly, so dramatically, that only God himself could mend these poor souls."

Then, the General visibly changed his posture and sat up taller in his chair, shoulders back.

"I'm a Christian, and darn proud to say so. I hope that doesn't offend anyone, and if it does, well, too bad. And I'll tell you this, if we've ever needed Jesus, it's right here, right now. I'm just an old soldier. I'm a fighter, and I understand the battlefield and military tactics better than anyone I know, and I've never lost a fight. I don't intend to lose this one. I'll tell you something else, I give you my solemn promise, that as your President, I will, with every fiber of my being, and every resource at my disposal, fight this enemy to my last breath, and I don't believe the good Lord is ready to take me home just yet, so that's not going to be anytime soon."

Mack looked at the handful of people in the room with him, and he noticed several of them dabbing at their eyes with a tissue, or with the back of their hand, or with a knuckle.

The General could command a room. It was one of his gifts, and one of the qualities that made him such an exceptional leader.

The sight of his colleagues moved him to an even stronger conviction.

"I know you must all be terribly afraid. I don't blame you one bit for that. As a combat soldier, I have been afraid more times than I can remember. But I'll tell you this: Fear keeps you alive, if you keep your head. The thing you cannot do, that you must not do, is allow your fear to cause you to panic and to make bad decisions. Keep your wits about you, think about your every move and ask yourself, will this move improve my situation? You've made it this far. There is no reason you cannot continue to survive until we, as a Nation, find a way to fight and win against this terrible enemy. Use your fear to keep you sharp and focused on what you have to do."

The General motioned to Angie for another glass of water. She brought it to him, and as she handed it to him, she held his gaze for a few moments. She wasn't sure she knew why, but she felt the compelling need to convey something to him. Angie guessed she was somehow trying to say thank you to the General for being so... so strong, so real. They desperately needed that right now. A true leader with strength and courage.

Somehow, Mack instinctively understood and patted her hand gently before proceeding.

"We are going to continue these broadcasts nightly, as long as it's safe for us to do so. Our next broadcast will be tomorrow, Friday evening, at about this same time. If we miss one, keep tuning in nightly. It's entirely possible that we may be forced to move to a new location from time to time. For now, please understand, please know, you are not in this alone. Throughout our great Nation, we have many surviving pockets of military and government personnel with which we have established channels of constant communication. Within our next few broadcasts, we will begin providing you with detailed updates and instructions. Until then, please do not engage anyone whom you suspect may be infected with this virus. You will most likely not survive such an encounter, not until we know what we're dealing with, and how to deal with it effectively."

He knew how to deal with them, *blow their damn heads off*, but he couldn't say that. Well, not yet.

"We need each and every one of you to stay alive, to help us rebuild our great Nation. There are far too few of us remaining. Please stay safe, please stay alive. God Bless you all, and may God Bless The United States of America."

Mack bowed his head and said a silent prayer. Then he slowly pushed his chair back and finally stood.

He really needed a glass of whisky.

Chapter 22

Luke and Archie

* * *

L uke stared at the radio in disbelief, mouth agape, as static filled the tinny sounding speaker. Then he heard a female voice interrupt the static momentarily.

"This recorded message will repeat at the top of each hour until our next live broadcast," she said. "Until then, stay safe and God Bless you all," she ended.

More static...

Luke's lower lip quivered. It was unexpected. He wiped the unexpected tears from his cheek. He suddenly felt very small. He suddenly felt very alone. Luke wanted, no, needed, Archie next to him. He whistled a quick sharp whistle and Archie came lumbering through the door, tail wagging. Luke patted his leg and Archie came next to him and sat down on his haunches, staring up at Luke.

"Hey Big Bear, Love you boy," Luke said with a little smile as he ruffled Archie's big soft head. Archie laid down at his master's feet, got comfortable, and closed his eyes. He did not know what was happening in the world, and was perfectly content to be with Luke, with his master, and nothing else mattered. Luke was Archie's entire world and was happy as long as they were together. Luke envied him so much at that moment. But at the same time, he was so very grateful for his companion. He could not imagine being here, now, in this moment, without his best friend.

"Thank you Lord Jesus," he uttered softly.

What he had just heard though, had made a bit more sense of everything he and Archie had been through... *How many days ago? He said the next broadcast would be on Friday night. That must mean it's Thursday!* They had been in this basement for 4 days already and Luke did not know that much time had passed. But it sort of made sense now, because he was feeling stronger, and his ankle and shoulder were feeling better. Time was a total mystery for them since his phone died. He hadn't even known what day it was until now. They had been living in complete isolation from the world until that broadcast.

"We're in a bit of a pickle, Big Bear. Seems that things are going to be a little different for a while. Well, a lot different. And we need to figure out what we're gonna do."

Then he cried out, "Katie!"

Archie looked up at him and gave a joyful bark from his laying position. Archie loved Kate, and whenever Luke said her name, Archie always got excited. That subtle affirmation from Archie was just what Luke needed to confirm what they were going to do. They had to get out of there. Get out and find Kate!

Luke wasn't a soldier, not even close, but he wasn't stupid either, and he understood the concept of stamina and endurance. He and Archie saw firsthand how dangerous those people were out there, and he knew that if they hoped to survive that madness outside the basement, they would be pushed to their limits. Archie seemed okay now, but Luke was still hurting. Though he was much better, he wasn't close to where he thought he needed to be, not to venture out there to face all that he knew must be waiting for them.

Luke just couldn't believe this was their new world now. They almost didn't make it down here to the basement alive, in his own house, a place he was more familiar with than anyplace in the world, and now he needed to go out there. Out there, there were far more unknowns, far more danger. He didn't want to go. Those... once-people had almost ended him and Archie, and from what he had just heard on the radio, there would be a lot more of them outside.

Luke continued just sitting there, looking down at Archie, so glad for his company, pondering their dilemma. Logic was one of Luke's defining qualities. He had always been a rational and clear thinker, and planning things came naturally to him. He could almost always tackle a problem methodically, and come out on top. But he had never faced anything like this before. He had never faced a life or death situation before. Not even close. But he could figure this out, couldn't he? He just needed to have a plan, a good plan, and he needed to get stronger.

Lifting his ankle, and laying it across his other leg as he sat there, he rolled it around with his hands. It was sore, but he could move it through just about its entire range of motion. He was glad. He knew time was short, and he wanted to leave as soon as possible.

"Hey boy, let's go get something to eat and start making some plans."

Bark! Bark!

Chapter 23

Luke's Journal

* * *

Luke made his way to the shelf next to the stove and pulled out two cans of SpaghettiOs with Meatballs, and two cans of Chunky Sirloin Burger soup. A pot and a large bowl were already waiting for him as he first opened the two cans of Chunky Soup for Archie. He hated feeding Archie food that probably wasn't all that good for him, but it was the best he could do, and Archie certainly didn't mind. Besides, he was thankful that they had food to eat at all.

Archie's baloney tongue was hanging out of his big, goofy face in anticipation of the tasty dinner he was about to get. Luke stared down at him as he held his bowl just out of reach.

"Hey boy, you're not hungry, are ya?" Luke teased. Archie barked loudly. It was a big bark from a big dog, and in this small space it seemed even bigger. "Are you sure? Because I can totally eat this if you don't want it."

Bark! Bark!

"Okay, okay, here ya go. Now don't eat it too fast because I still have to heat mine up, and I don't want to eat alone," Luke said light-heartedly. He knew it would be gone in about 10 seconds, but he loved joking around with Archie, even though he knew his pup had no idea what he was saying. That was okay, though. The tone of his voice and the smile on his face conveyed love to Archie, and he knew he understood that. Luke plopped two can-shaped blobs of old SpaghettiOs into the pot and watched as they melted into a delicious-smelling gourmet meal. He was dreaming of the taste while he waited. And while he waited, he watched his furry best friend. Archie had long since finished his Chunky Soup, and had already begun licking the insides of all four cans that Luke placed on the floor for him to clean. His long tongue easily reached the bottom of each and it was fun to watch Archie go to work on them and then play with them once they were all clean and shiny inside.

After chowing down on his own large portion of SpaghettiOs, Luke washed his pot and Archie's bowl, then went to his bunk and picked up the small journal he'd found and claimed for his own. He began writing. He titled the first page, *Kate,* and next to that he wrote the date: *November 10th, 2022.*

Luke figured the most important thing he had to do right now was to get stronger so that he and Archie could get out of the basement to go find her. He knew what was out there, and there was no way he was going to leave the safety of Grandpa's bunker until he knew he could outrun those things. And he didn't for a moment think that he wouldn't have to. He would just have to push himself as hard as he could over the next few days.

As he held his journal thoughtfully, he wrote:

* * *

I think it's Thursday. The radio said it was, but I may have been listening to a recording. I have no way to know for sure because my phone is somewhere upstairs with those half human, half dead things up there. Mostly dead, I think. Anyway, Archie and I are okay now.

We found Grandpa's bunker down in the basement. We barely made it down here. I'm hurt, but not too badly. My ankle is the worst, but it's healing, and it's already much better than it was when we finally got that door closed at the top of the stairs. That was 4 days ago, I think. I sprained my ankle, and I also got a pretty nasty cut on my shoulder, but otherwise I'm okay. Archie seems fine now. He got tossed around quite a bit before we made it down here and I thought I lost him a couple of times, but he's a lot tougher than I am and he seems okay now. Just like his old self.

I'm not sure why I'm writing this, but I think it's important to keep track of time and what we're going through. Maybe someday it will help us in some way, or perhaps someone else. Who knows... Anyway, we need to get out of this basement and go find Kate as soon as we can. I'm not ready yet though. My ankle is still pretty sore. We're safe down here for now, and we have plenty of food and water. Grandpa really stocked up with enough supplies to get through World War III. I didn't even know what he'd done until we were forced down here to get away from those things. That heavy steel door and steel cross bar to lock it has kept them out so far, and I don't think they can get in.

Those things? I think they are, well, I can't think of anything else to call them but zombies. Yea, I said zombies, just like in those undead stories and movies. I feel crazy even thinking it, more crazy writing it, and maybe I am, but I swear, they aren't human anymore and they smell horrible. And after running into several that got into the house, I'm convinced that their only purpose was to eat me. Some sure tried. The first was Mrs. Benson standing outside the downstairs window, her throat missing, but still somehow alive and trying to scream. I'll never forget her eyes. I could see her terror as she stared at me, pleading with me through the glass. Then there was the circus-like fat man that got inside the house. I don't know who he was, but he was the fattest man I'd ever seen and he had a sort of black oily ooze coming out of him. He was almost the end of me, but Archie saved me. I mean, really saved me from a certain end from that one. He'd save me even more times before we'd make it safely down to Grandpa's basement bunker. Then there was Kansas City, then the creepy, ghouly family trio. But I think the worst of all was Gus. It was Gus; it had to be Gus. I'd recognize him anywhere. But it wasn't Gus any more. He was the last one we got away from just before we slammed and barred the basement door shut. Is he still up there? I don't know. For what seemed like forever, he was pounding and moaning against the door. But then it just suddenly stopped, and I haven't heard anything since. Except for those booms, the ones that sounded like gunshots. But I don't know what that was. And I can't remember when Gus stopped banging. Was it before or after those booms? I don't know, my mind's fuzzy on that one. But what I did figure out was that the only way I could stop them was to shoot them in the head. Shooting them anywhere else just seemed to anger them more, if that was even possible. I think that's important. Archie ripped the spine out of one just below its head from behind. That was the fat man that was on top of me. That sure stopped that one.

After making it down here, I discovered all that Gramps had done. There were first aid supplies, food, water, a shower, a toilet, even lights down here, that are powered by solar somehow. Even a bunk room. Gramps also put in a gas stove that actually works. He thought of everything. I'm so thankful. I miss him more now than ever. Gramps, I love you.

I'm patched up now and healing some. I think we've been down here for four days or so, but I'm not sure. I found a radio that Gramps stored down here and I heard, well; it was either a recording or a live broadcast, I don't know which, but it was by a General McPherson. He said he was the Secretary of Defense. I should know that, but I don't. Politics was never really my thing. He said he was now the President of the United States. He said some sort of weaponized viral attack caused all this and it's all across the Country. I'm going to try to catch the next broadcast, if there is one, and I'll write more about that then. I don't know anything else right now.

I found a notebook that Grandpa left behind. It was as if he knew something bad was going to happen. I haven't read it all yet, because it was full of instructions about the bunker. But he also wrote a letter and put it at the front of the notebook. I did read that, twice. It's as if he were right here with me and talking to me. I sure do miss him.

I've decided our next move is to go look for Kate. We talked on the phone just after Mrs. Benson hit our window downstairs, but then I lost my phone when more of them got inside. She was okay then. But until I find my phone, I have no way of reaching her. It's upstairs somewhere. I'll find it when I'm ready to face those things again. And I will be ready this time. Well, as ready as I can be, I mean. Gramps has plenty of guns and ammo down here.

Right now, I need to get stronger and get this ankle feeling better. I'm going to make out a P.T. schedule and fast track it until I drop. When I know I'm okay to leave, we're outta here. Hang in there, Katie, I'm coming to get you, baby. Please be okay until I do. I love you. I do.

Archie barked and gave Luke that, *I gotta go,* look. "Okay boy, let's go do that, then we'll get started!"

Bark!

Luke wrote one last entry in his journal and then stood up.

Lord, I really need you. Please help us. Please keep Archie and me safe so we can find Katie. Any help you can give us along the way would mean a lot. I love you Father, Amen.

Chapter 24

P.T.

* * *

Luke knew he had no time to waste if he had any hope of finding Katie. *Am I already too late?*

"No, I can't think like that. Kate is okay. She's smart, and she's strong. I know she's okay, I just know it."

Bark!

At the sound of Kate's name, Archie perked up and let out a sharp bark.

"We need to get out of here, boy," Luke said as he ruffled the top of Archie's head. "First, though, we have some work to do."

He thought about the training Coach Harris tortured his team with before a big game. He called it game-readiness PT, but it was more like a contest to see who could puke the most. Luke hated those 2-hour PT sessions. Coach held them during the extended athletics period each school day during football season, and by the time they made it to the field for actual football practice after school, the team was already wiped out. But somehow, they always dug deep and found their second wind that the coach knew they had. Luke's team had won the State Championship three of his four years in high school, and he knew it was because of how hard Coach had pushed them, how he trained them. Jonah ate it up, but Luke hated it. Jonah always made things look so easy, though.

Luke thought for a moment about Jonah and hoped he was okay. Then he smiled to himself and looked at Archie again. He knew that if anyone could make it through this nightmare, Jonah was the one to do it.

There wasn't a lot of room in the basement, but there was a path between the bathroom and the back wall just past the stove that was about a 30-foot run. Luke had to move the table and chairs over a few feet, closer to the stove, but he could make this work.

"Okay, ready, boy?"

Bark! Bark!

"Let's go!"

Luke bolted forward and raced Archie to the back wall. Archie hopped up and down like a giddy puppy the whole way, looking playfully up at Luke the entire time, with his tongue hanging out, wondering what this fun new game was. Luke, on the other hand, was gritting his teeth through the pain in his ankle, but he didn't stop. They sprinted 10 times back and forth as fast as Luke could go, paying attention to not change direction too fast and risk re-injuring his ankle. At each end, Luke would touch the ground, and then run back the other way. *Good ole fashioned wind-sprints*, Coach Harris called them. Luke counted each time he touched the floor, and when he got to 20, he dropped, gasping for air, ankle aching. Archie was still hopping around Luke, not showing the least bit of fatigue.

"Yeah, well, you've got four legs boy, I've only got two. And one of those isn't working too well right now," Luke panted out over several seconds and several heaving breaths.

After a minute or two, Luke sat up and crossed his left leg over his right, and began rolling and stretching his sore ankle. He was sure to hold each stretch as long as he could bear it. He did this for a few minutes, and it felt a little better each time. Then Luke got up and repeated his sprinting drill several more times, followed by stretching his ankle again. He lost count, but he was sure he'd pushed his ankle as hard as he should for now. Archie had long since given up on the chasing game and plopped down on the floor with his face between his front paws, lips splayed flat out on the floor, just watching Luke as if he were doing it all wrong. His eyes were almost accusing Luke of not paying enough attention to him during the chase. Archie loved playing chase and keep away with Luke, but this was boring and he didn't want anymore to do with it.

After a particularly long break of laying on the floor, Luke finally got up and said, "Let's get some water, and then something to eat. How does that sound, Big Bear?"

Bark! Bark!

Lunch consisted of several cans of StarKist Chunk Light Tuna in water, and a half a box of stale Ritz Crackers. Gramps had sealed the crackers, box and all, in some sort of vacuum packed bag with all the air sucked out, but Luke didn't mind at all. Besides, he thought they sure tasted good with the tuna. They ate four cans each.

After cleaning up their small mess, Luke began his next round. This time it was pushups, sit-ups, and calf-raises. Luke did 54 pushups before his arms went all wobbly, then he did 70 sit-ups, and then managed to eke out 20 calf-raises before his ankle said, *No more, please!* But then, after a brief rest, he repeated the exercises. Each set diminished the number he could do. When he got down to maxing out at 10, he had had enough. He was sore all over, but it sure felt good that he was doing something. And Luke knew this was something he had to do.

Luke felt bad for Archie. He loved his pup and would spend two or three hours every day playing ball, training, going on long hikes, or on a jog together. But being cooped up down here in the basement for how many days now? Three? Four maybe? He could tell Archie was more than ready to leave this place.

As Luke stood under the hot shower, he looked down at Archie

166

sprawled out on the bathroom floor near the sink. Then he had an idea. He just hoped it would work!

Putting on a fresh t-shirt and a pair of sweatpants from Grandpa's clothing stash made Luke think of getting in bed for a good night's sleep, but he had to try out his idea first. He needed to do this for Archie. So, on his way out of the bathroom, Luke grabbed a small washcloth and headed for the bookshelf by the stairway leading up. It was on the same shelf where he found Grandpa's shotgun.

"There you are," Luke said as he picked up the roll of duct tape. Luke took the roll of tape and the small washcloth and sat down at the table and went to work. Within just a couple of minutes, Luke had fashioned a nice, tight ball with the washcloth wadded up on the inside and duct tape wrapped all around it on the outside. It was about the size of an orange, but it was light, and felt pretty sturdy. He pressed it and formed it in his hands as much as he could, to make it as round as possible. He got it pretty close. "This just might do the trick," Luke smiled to himself, satisfied with the new toy.

"Hey boy, wanna play ball?"

That was one word Archie knew better than any other, and he came tearing out of the bathroom from where he'd been laying on the floor the entire time Luke was working on his homemade ball. Archie had the happiest look on his face that Luke had seen in a long while. Luke threw the make-shift ball at the far wall, at the back of his indoor wind-sprint track, and it bounced almost as well as the squeaky tennis balls he'd get at the pet store. Archie flew after it and looked so silly trying to grab hold of it as it bounced here and there. When he finally figured out the weight and feel of the new ball, he chomped down on it, trying to squeak it as he brought it back to Luke. Of course, it didn't squeak, but Archie didn't seem to mind at all. It was all covered in slobber too, and he made Luke wrestle it away from him to give it another throw.

"Yuck dude, now I know why they don't make the squeaky balls from the pet store out of this stuff. At least those soak up most of the drool," Luke said in mock disgust. But it delighted him that the ball worked even better than he'd hoped it would. Archie loved his new toy, and Luke must have tossed that ball for an hour with Archie, and as he did, he realized it was great conditioning for his pup, too. Archie was as his old self again and filled with joy to play ball with his master.

Loud banging on the door at the top of the stairs, followed by inhuman moaning, began unexpectedly, and startled both of them. Archie stopped in his tracks, mid-way back to Luke with the makeshift ball. They both stared at the dark stairway and just stood there, frozen for a few long moments. The banging and moaning increased in intensity, and Luke realized that their energetic play had most likely agitated whatever was up there.

Whatever was up there... Luke knew exactly what was up there. He also knew they'd have to face it soon.

Archie started to bristle and growl.

"Shhh boy," Luke whispered. "I think our playing woke them up. Let's try to be quiet for a while."

Luke made his way over to Archie and began stroking him behind his ears to calm him a bit, but Archie remembered what was up there, too. Luke could see it in his eyes and in his posture. He led Archie to the bunk room and, as quietly as he could, he closed the door. The banging continued, but more muffled now with the door closed. He and Archie heard it just the same, though. It was time for bed, but as tired as he was, Luke knew there would be little sleep for him that night.

Luke got into his bunk and slid between the cool white sheets, and man was he thankful for his bunk. "Goodnight, boy," Luke whispered, and patted Archie on the top of his head as he stood right next to Luke's bunk. Archie licked Luke's face in reply. "Yeah, I love you too Big Bear".

Luke said a quick prayer and dropped into a deep sleep.

Chapter 25

The Visitor

* * *

Bang! Bang! Bang!

Three rapid gunshots ripped Luke out of his deep slumber, followed by Archie growling next to his head. Luke shot up and reached for Archie, nuzzling his face to calm him a bit. It was quiet for a few moments, but then there was a scream, a girl's scream, followed by more silence, then a single gunshot and another scream. Someone was in his house, and it sounded like a young girl.

"Someone's in real trouble up there, boy," Luke whispered, as he spun around and put his feet on the floor, and turned on the small table lamp. "We have to help."

Archie stared at the door leading out of their bunk room. "It'll be okay, boy, we're gonna go help her." Luke rose and got dressed. He put his belt on, which held a holstered government issue Colt 1911, and an OD green dual mag carrier pouch that held two 7-round magazines for the old Colt. Grandpa had 4 of these prized pistols in the gun safe, and 4 of the green military belts, as well as some old leather holsters that had a large flap that covered the pistol. Luke found a more modern Kydex holster with an open top for quicker access and picked that one instead. Luke put on his boots and grabbed the old Mossberg 12-Gauge pump shotgun leaning against the wall, and opened the bunk room door. Archie was next to Luke, pressed against his leg, but was eager to get up those stairs. Luke had never seen this courageous side of his loyal companion before, not until this madness started. He had read about how heroic and fierce some German Shepherds were, and how protective they could be, but to him, Archie was just his big goofy best friend. He never really saw him as a protector. This event, though, whatever it was, brought out a different side of Archie. One that must have always been there, but needed a catalyst to trigger those generations of buried instincts within him.

"We're going to take it slow and easy, boy," Luke whispered. "Stay next to me."

Luke approached the stairs leading up, Archie right by his side, listening as they inched forward. There were no more gunshots, no more screaming or banging, or anything like that, but there was something... something faint, something indiscernible from where he and Archie were standing at the bottom of the stairs. Archie detected it too, because his ears were pointed straight up, eyes glued to the darkness at the top of the stairs.

One step, then two, then three, quietly, methodically. Halfway up now, and Luke stopped and switched on the flashlight he had taped to the side of the Mossberg. With the stairway washed in bright light now, he wished he had turned it on when they were at the bottom of the stairs, instead of waiting until they were halfway up. Within a few moments, they had reached the landing just behind the barred door. Archie started sniffing at the crack at the base of the door, and Luke couldn't hear anything except for the racket Archie was making. "Big Bear, quiet, I can't hear anything, shhh," Luke softly commanded. After one or two more sniffs, Archie sat at Luke's feet, and Luke pressed his ear to the door. At first, Luke couldn't hear anything at all, but then he did. It was like a soft girl's voice, singing maybe? No, crying. It sounded like there was a small girl sitting on the other side of the door, softly crying.

"I'm going to open the door, boy. Someone on the other side needs our help. Stay," Luke commanded. Archie looked up at his master with obvious concern in his eyes.

Luke lifted the large locking bar and put his hand on the door handle. He listened once again with his ear to the door, and when there was nothing, he made a silent count in his head.

One, two, three...

The basement door swung open an inch or two, and Luke released the door handle. The natural light that came through the crack surprised him. That was a sight he and Archie hadn't seen in days. He pressed the button on the small flashlight attached to the shotgun to turn it off. The crying had stopped with the opening of the door, but then a small voice said, "Who's there?"

Archie did not wait for the okay from his master. Instead, at the sound of that small voice, Archie pushed his nose into the crack of the door, and wedged it the rest of the way open, until it stopped with a dull thump. It was less than halfway open, but that's as far as it would go. It was enough, though, for Archie to squeeze through and find his target.

The young girl's eyes filled with terror at the sight of the large German Shepherd bounding right toward her, but she was too slow in bringing her hands up to protect herself. Archie was already on her and got right in her face and began licking her and whining playfully. The relief in the girl's eyes, and in her expression, was instant. She brought her hands up the rest of the way and began kneading her small fingers into the soft fur on both sides of Archies's large fluffy face.

"Oh, you're a friendly dog," she said in a small quivering voice. She was still clearly distraught, but she was no longer crying. And there even seemed to be a small smile in her words as she tried to get some air, in-between Archie's kisses.

As Luke made his way through the door, he assessed the area as fast as he could, to look for any danger that might be near. There were a lot of bodies on the floor, but there was one in particular that caught Luke's attention. It was blocking the entry into the mudroom and basement door area. He had almost lost his and Archie's life to that behemoth. "Gus," Luke said softly to himself. He looked at Gus for a long moment to make sure he was really dead. Gus still didn't move, and there was an enormous hole in his forehead and it looked like half of his skull was missing. Gus was indeed dead. Luke turned his attention to the young girl, where Archie had most definitely found a new friend, and Luke noticed a large handgun laying on the ground next to her leg. It reminded him of one his best friend, Jonah, had. It was a unique-looking pistol, and he had never seen one before, other than Jonah's.

"That's Archie," Luke said in the most upbeat voice he could muster. He knew the young girl must be terribly afraid, and he didn't want to frighten her more. "He likes you," Luke added. The girl just buried her face into Archies' fur around his neck. Luke knew exactly what that felt like because he loved to give Archie hugs when they were playing together. "I know you're afraid, but you don't have to be afraid of me, or Archie, okay? My name is Luke, and this is my house." Before Luke could ask the girl's name, Archie turned away from the girl suddenly, and stood rigidly with his ears pointed straight up again. He was staring past Gus into the hall leading to the kitchen. He didn't move, didn't flinch, but then there was a crashing sound coming from the kitchen.

"We have to go now, okay? Right now, come with me please!" Luke commanded.

It surprised him that the girl got up so quickly, practiced even, as if she was fully aware of the danger and the importance of his words and the need to move.

"Archie, come!" He commanded, but Archie would not leave the girl's side. As she moved, Archie heeled right next to *her*, and Luke recognized right away that Archie was protecting the little girl.

More crashing sounds, then the horrible familiar groaning sound followed. Luke reached for the girl, but she just ran past him, with Archie still glued to her side.

It was a serious situation, but Luke couldn't help whispering, "Traitor," to himself with a half-smile, as the two bolted through the basement door. Luke turned to go back through the door, and as he did, he saw a large body laying across the floor just behind it. That was the thing blocking the door from opening all the way. There was something familiar about it, but Luke didn't waste a second longer getting through and pulling the door closed hard behind him. Once closed, he dropped the large crossbar into place.

In that same span of time, Archie and the girl were already down the stairs. Then, Luke heard the little girl say, "Your name is Archie."

Bark! Bark!

"My name is Sophia, but Jonah called me Cricket. I sorta liked it."

Archie licked Sophia's face.

To be continued...

V.I.P. Club

Building a relationship with my readers is the very best thing about writing. You cannot imagine how terribly important that is to me. I occasionally send newsletters with details on my new releases, special offers, free copies of the Audiobook versions of my Novels (Audible) and other bits of news relating to the Luke's Apocalypse series, and other titles and series I'm working on. And if you sign up to my mailing list you'll not only have the opportunity to receive free copies of my books and audiobooks, you'll also sometimes be offered the chance to participate in my plot and story structure ideas, beta readership program, and many other fun events.

Please go here to signup. I'd love to meet you!

https://www.apshepherd.com/v-i-p-club

I will never share your email address or spam you with unwanted email and you can opt out easily at any time.

- tiktok.com/@apshepherd
- amazon.com/stores/A.P.-Shepherd/author/B0BW5C8F8T? ref=ap_rdr&store_ref=ap_rdr&isDramIntegrated=true&shoppingPortalEnabled=true

Your Review Means Everything!

Did you enjoy this book? You can make an unbelievable difference!

Your review means more than you may know. Reviews are truly the lifeblood for me as an independent author. I read each and every review and am so thankful for all of them - good and bad.

It only takes a moment ~ and it means so very much!

Navigate to your purchase of Luke's Apocalypse
https://www.amazon.com
Look for the "Write a Customer Review" button.

Thank You and God Bless, A.P.

About A.P. Shepherd

A.P Shepherd is an exciting new Post Apocalyptic Survival Thriller Author - with his breakout debut series: Luke's Apocalypse.

He make's his online home here: https://www.apshepherd.com

Should you like to contact A.P. Directly via email - you can reach him here: ap@apshepherd.com

www.ingramcontent.com/pod-product-compliance
Lightning Source LLC
Chambersburg PA
CBHW050848180626
46814CB00007B/2673